T

The Sands of Karakorum is a step by James Ramsey Ullman into a new dimension of writing—and one of the most unusual novels of this, or any other, season.

In its outer framework it is a tale of movement, of suspense, of search. John and Eleanor Bickel, American missionaries, have vanished into the maw of Red China, and Frank Knight, in the dual role of old friend and newspaper correspondent, sets out to find them. The trail leads darkly, tortuously, from Shanghai through the obscure byways of interior China and on into the remote heartland of Central Asia. It ends—or almost ends—in the "desert of the black sands," where lie the ruins of Karakorum, the ancient capital of Genghis Khan.

The Sands of Karakorum, however, is far more than the account of a mere physical journey. And its "search" is for more than two individuals who are lost. Exactly what it is that Frank Knight and the Bickels seek—and find— is a matter which each reader will have to decide for himself.

It is a story of mood and emotion, of tension and mounting terror and deep imaginative power. But, above all, it is a story of man's faith and hope in the wasteland of a darkened world. His fable of the black sands, says Mr. Ullman, has haunted him for many years. Now that he has at last set it down, it should haunt many another as well—long after (like Frank Knight) he has turned the last page and put out the light.

J. B. LIPPINCOTT COMPANY

Philadelphia   New York

THE SANDS OF KARAKORUM

James Ramsey Ullman

133 $\frac{1830}{147}$

To

Godfather

Books by James Ramsey Ullman

THE SANDS OF KARAKORUM

ISLAND OF THE BLUE MACAWS

WINDOM'S WAY

RIVER OF THE SUN

THE WHITE TOWER

HIGH CONQUEST: The Story of Mountaineering

THE OTHER SIDE OF THE MOUNTAIN: An Escape to the Amazon

MAD SHELLEY

KINGDOM OF ADVENTURE: EVEREST (Editor)

Have pity upon me . . . O ye my friends;
for the hand of God hath touched me.

Job, 19:21

The Sands of Karakorum

It is all right until the wind blows.

I do my work. I go my rounds. I make my phone calls and get my interviews and file my cable, and the next day the by-line, *by Frank Knight*, appears in fifty-odd newspapers from Vermont to Texas. Now the cable is from Japan; now from Korea, Hong Kong, Indo-China, Malaya. Except for China, my beat is the same as ever. The world is as fouled up as ever. My life is the same as ever.

Until the wind blows.

Until it is night and I am alone in my hotel room at the typewriter, trying to sort the day's confused grist into the neat precision of words; and then some-times, in the darkness beyond the window, I hear the sound of the wind. It is always a low sound, deep and humming, and seeming to be a part of the darkness. And on those nights I raise my head and listen; I leave my typewriter and turn off the light and lie on my bed, listening; and soon everything else is gone—my work, my life, the world itself, all gone and lost—and that is all there is: the darkness and the wind.

It is only the fever, I think. Only the old fever again, the residue of typhus stirring in my blood. But in the next instant I am not sure. I listen, and the wind hums, and the humming seems a thing of my own body and brain. But then, suddenly, it has changed. It is outside me, beyond me. It flows into the room from the night beyond; from the night over the city, the night over the land. It comes to me from a great distance, across a sea and a continent, across the mountains and the deserts, from the deep heart of Asia.

I try to sleep. But there is no sleep. There is only the wind and the dark and, beyond them, the two faint figures that are John and Eleanor Bickel. . . . Receding. Receding. But never gone. . . . And pres-ently I get up and go back to the typewriter, but this time it is not to write a dispatch. It is to tell their story. Perhaps, by setting it down, I can exorcise them, forget them. Or perhaps—and this would be better—it will bring me at last to an understanding of what they have done and where they have gone.

But, whatever the outcome, it is a story that I must tell.

At least the clicking keys hold back the sound of the wind.

North Station, Shanghai. June of 1950.

There were still Americans in Shanghai then. Not many. But a few. Although the Communists had held the city for more than a year, they had taken their time in cleaning out the foreign colony, concentrating first on the big proprietors, agents and bankers and leaving the smaller fry until last. In that late spring of '50 perhaps a thousand Americans were left: a nucleus of teachers and missionaries; a scattering of clerks, salesmen, technicians, professional men; a handful of correspondents. And I was one of them.

Not that there was much for a newspaperman to

do, for the Bamboo Curtain was already high and thick. My dispatches were censored down almost to the prepositions and conjunctions. But my syndicate felt that even a gagged correspondent was better than no correspondent and had told me to stay on as long as I could. At least when I was put out—which might well be any month, or week, or day—I would have a backlog of experience and observation that would be useful for the future.

That was the theory, and I stayed on. I went my rounds and made my calls and wrangled with commissars and wrangled with censors and drank too many pink gins and played poker at night at what was left of the Press Club. And on a bright June morning in "The Year of Liberation, 2" I went to the North Station to meet a train.

Partly it was job; for the train was bringing a load of missionaries whom the Reds had expelled from one of the interior provinces, and the story warranted covering, whatever the censor might subsequently do to it. But even more it was a personal affair, for among the refugees, I was certain, would be the Bickels. . . . John, Eleanor, their daughter Jean. . . . Jean would be—what?—almost twelve now, I figured, as my pedicab threaded the narrow streets near the station. I had not seen the Bickels for more than two years.

As soon as I heard of the missionary train I had called the Shanghai headquarters of their society.

Would they be on it? I asked.

Yes, they were expecting them.

Had they heard from Bickel?

Not directly, no. Communications with the interior were terrible. But the train was supposed to be bringing everyone from Honan Province, and that would of course include them.

So now I was at the station. Outside, the swarming square: crowds in blue cotton tunics; oxcarts and pedicabs and coolies with their loads and shoulder-poles; sleek American cars carrying officials and American jeeps and trucks carrying soldiers; children playing, peddlers clanking their bells; heat, dust, smells. Inside, a dingy cavern, more crowds, posters of Mao and Chu Te; then clouds of steam, an engine panting. From long experience I had timed it right in being two hours late, and the refugee train was just pulling in. Clustered at the gate were the remnants of the clerical population of Shanghai, waiting to greet their colleagues. In China, as elsewhere, the First and Fourth Estates inhabited very different worlds, and I saw only a few vaguely familiar faces. Whether any of them was from Bickel's society I didn't know.

The train had stopped. The crowd tightened. Guards, trainmen and officials were moving about the platform. Then a whistle blew, the coach doors opened, and the refugees began descending and moving toward us. It was a strange and bizarre procession. First came a group of gray-robed nuns, then two aged priests carried on coolies' backs, then a file of Chinese Trappist monks, moving silently with downcast eyes. There were other Chinese, Americans, Englishmen, Frenchmen, Italians; Catholics, Anglicans, Methodists, Baptists, Adventists. There were young rawboned men in boots and khaki, old frail men with umbrellas and paper suitcases, women in robes and women in homemade print dresses, carrying knapsacks on their backs and babies in their arms. There was, in cross-section, the whole missionary world of China, and I would scarcely have been surprised if one of the coach doors had opened suddenly to disgorge the Twelve Apostles.

Yet, for all its variety, it was not a colorful procession. It was drab. It was slow-footed. Even the children walked slowly and silently, holding tightly to their parents' hands. They had spent the night—and God knows how many previous nights—on the wooden benches of the train; and they were tired, bone tired. But there was also something beyond tiredness, something deeper than tiredness, that showed in their gait, their bodies, their faces, their eyes. It was a trancelike somnambulistic quality, the same that I had seen a hundred times over, for fifteen years, in the barracks and queues and waiting rooms and wire cages of the gray half-world of the refugee. The Book of Exodus, I thought: Shanghai, A.D. 1950. Without a Moses to lead them, they came down the platform and through the gate, in the slow straggling march of the uprooted and the homeless.

I watched for the Bickels. Even in a crowd much larger than this John Bickel's six-foot-three would be easy to spot, and I stood a little back from the press at the gate, waiting for him to appear. But he did not appear. The procession flowed on, dwindled, ended. A one-legged Carmelite friar limped through, supported by two of his brothers; and that was the last of it. The Bickels were not there.

The refugees were being herded into one of the smaller waiting rooms, and, along with the others who had come to meet them, I followed them in. It was a low-ceilinged airless place, full of confusion, smells and piles of battered baggage, and for a few minutes I wandered about aimlessly. Off to one side the Chinese Trappists squatted motionless against a wall. Near them, on a bench, six nuns sat in a row, absorbed in their rosaries. Here and there were knots of animation, handclasps, greetings. Those with no one to meet them stood patiently waiting. . . . For what? . . . Somewhere a thin reedy voice began singing *Jesus Loves Me*. Soon a few others joined in.

My eye fell on a man standing alone—youngish, alert-looking, obviously American—and I went over and spoke to him.

"Do you know John Bickel?" I asked.

He repeated the name and shook his head. "From Honan?" he said.

"Yes."

"What district?"

"A town called Sanchow."

"Sanchow is in the far west of the province. I am from the east. I have never been there."

I tried others, but with little more result. Most of them were from eastern Honan, around the capital city of Kaifeng. A few had heard Bickel's name, but knew nothing about him. "It has not been like in the old days," said one, "when we could move about freely through the country. For the past year we have been like prisoners, each in our own mission."

On my rounds I picked up fragments of stories that I might or might not be permitted to use in a dispatch. Stories of house arrest, prison arrest, of intimidation, persecution, execution. One Italian priest had been jailed without trial for six months on a charge of giving medical supplies to non-Communists. Another—an Irishman—had been tied to a stake and forced to watch while three of his Chinese assistants had been beheaded, for "espionage." And so on. Perhaps the saddest part of their sad stories was that they were all so similar, and so familiar. In the Year of The Red Star, 1950, they were no longer even news.

Did any of them know John Bickel?

No.

Had any been to Sanchow?

No.

An official had come into the room and was seated at a table, checking off names as the refugees passed before him.

"Do you have a Bickel?" I asked him.

He looked up at me in annoyance.

"Bickel." I spelled it.

He glanced through his list. "No, there is no Bickel."

"You're sure?"

"Look for yourself."

"Is there another train coming?"

"From Honan?" he said. "No, there is no other train from Honan. All the priests and such from Honan are on this train."

"All?"

"Yes, all."

I started to go, changed my mind, and stood near him while the refugees filed by. . . . Fra Augustino Ruffo, Franciscan, from Kaifeng. . . . The Reverend T. M. McPherson, Glasgow Missionary Society, Siping. . . . Lay Brother Vainu Riholuoma, Evangelical Church of Finland, Mingkiang. . . . Sister Theresa Anna Vospenska, Carmelite, Kaifeng. . . .

A dozen more went by.

. . . Archibald Granger, Society of Friends, Kioshan. . . . Father Anton Naganyi, Order of Preachers, Sanchow. . . .

He was a small man, a wisp of a man, with a white haunted face and skeletal hands. He wore shell-rimmed glasses with broken frames patched with adhesive tape. The white habit of his order was soiled and threadbare, and on his feet were torn blue tennis sneakers.

When he had passed the official I stepped up to him. He was a Central European, I was sure. Probably Hungarian. I spoke to him in Chinese.

"Where is John Bickel?" I asked.

He stared at me, as if he had not understood.

"The Bickels," I said. "From Sanchow. Where are they?"

He shook his head slowly. "They are not here."

"Why not? Where are they?"

"They did not come."

The priest made as if to move on, but I stopped him. "Why didn't they come?" I persisted. "What's happened to them?"

"I do not know," he said. "I have not seen them for many months."

"They were in Sanchow, weren't they?"

"Yes."

"And you too?"

"Only until six months ago. Then I was made to leave and sent to our house in Kaifeng."

"And the Bickels—weren't *they* made to leave?"

He shook his head.

"Why not?" I asked.

"I do not know," he said.

"But if you were both there—"

"Even in the beginning I saw little of Mr. Bickel. I am a Catholic. I had my own work, with my own people. And he had his. Then, after the new government came, I was under house arrest and could see no one."

"You must have heard about him. . . . Something."

The priest's eyes met mine for an instant, pale and flickering behind the glasses. Then he looked away. "No," he murmured, "I heard nothing. I know nothing."

The line of refugees moved past us. A child had begun to cry. Over in the corner they were singing *Rock of Ages*.

"All right, Father," I said. I touched his arm, and under the sleeve of his habit it seemed no more than a bare bone. "If you can't tell me, you can't. What about the others here? Is there anyone who would know?"

"No," he said. "There is no one."

"Anyone anywhere?"

He hesitated.

"Please, Father—"

"There is one who might know," he said at last. "He is—"

"Yes?"

"He is the former mayor of Sanchow. He knew Mr. Bickel better than I, and also he stayed on after I had gone. But I have heard he has since come to Shanghai."

"Where can I find him?"

Again the priest hesitated. His pale eyes searched my face. Then he said:

"You are from Mr. Bickel's society?"

"No. I am his friend."

"An American?"

"Yes."

"And not a—"

"No," I said, "not a Communist."

"Then—" He made his decision. "You have a pencil?" he asked. "Some paper?"

I gave them to him, and he wrote quickly and nervously. "Here," he said. "Here is the name and an address. I do not know that he is in Shanghai, you understand? I have only heard so. And if he is, he may be elsewhere. This is the home of his brother, and once, when I came here, I delivered a message for him." He returned the pencil and paper. "That is all I know. All I can tell you. But perhaps—"

A bell rang. The official had risen from the table. Guards began herding the crowd from the room.

"—perhaps, if he is there," the priest said, "he can tell you what you wish to know."

A guard tapped his shoulder and pointed. He picked up an umbrella and cardboard suitcase and moved away.

"Thank you, Father," I said.

I put paper and pencil in my pocket and went out by another door. Behind me, through the street noises, I could still hear the child crying and the voices singing:

> Rock of ages
> Cleft for me . . .

That was the beginning.

THREE

I am aware that an explanation is in order. In almost the same breath I have said that missionaries and correspondents live in different worlds and indicated that I was the close friend of a missionary family. That both happen to be true is what made my relationship with the Bickels so extraordinary.

Even the circumstances of our first meeting had been unusual. It had been back in 1937—my second year in the East—when I was stationed in Peiping, and one day, in need of exercise, I had gone to the YMCA for a game of handball. My opponent was to have been a chap called Lasker, of the United Press; but he didn't show up, and I had been about to leave when a tall redheaded man appeared and asked if I would like to play. Glad to, I told him, and we went at it. He was big-boned, slow-footed, a little awkward, and at first I had the notion that I was well within my class. The illusion was short-lived, however. Speed or no speed, wherever I hit the ball he was there waiting for it, and a split-second later it was banging back at me as if shot from a gun. He took the first game, 21-9, and the second, 21-6. Then in the third he merely went through the motions and I won by two points.

"Thanks for the charity," I told him.

"No, you were hitting your stride there," he assured me. "All you need is some practice."

We showered and dressed, and he put on ordinary street clothes, and I had him marked down as a businessman or perhaps an engineer for one of the oil companies. Then, out in the street, I suggested a drink, but he declined with thanks.

"Better not tonight," he explained. "I've a service coming up."

"Service?"

"At the mission. We have one every Thursday, and then a sort of party for the younger people."

"Oh."

He saw my reaction and smiled. "Another time, though, I'd be glad to," he said. "If you'd care to play again, that is."

"Why—of course."

"Don't worry, I won't try to convert you. Unless you ask for it."

"You can start off," I grinned, "by converting my handball."

So we played twice a week for perhaps a month, and though nothing much happened to my handball, at least my waist went down from 36 to 34. After the second session we did have a drink, and after a few others as well, and in the process we began to get acquainted. It was a gradual process, for John Bickel was not a man to open up quickly; and also, there was the great gap between our lives, work and interests. He knew no one I knew, rarely visited downtown Peiping, and was wholly unfamiliar with the hotels, clubs and restaurants that were the cosmopolitan center of the city. And I, for my part, had never heard of the district, much less the street, in which his mission was located.

Yet from the very beginning I liked his company. There was an attraction. A pull. He was about my own age (which was then in the early thirties), showed none of the bloodless stuffiness that I had always associated with his calling, and talked intelligently about everything from the cooking of noodles to press censorship and the Japs in Manchuria to big league baseball. His speech, like his movements, was slow and deliberate. There was in him no vestige of the frenetic restlessness that was the occupational disease of my own profession. But neither was there heaviness or dullness. The soft voice, the clear gray eyes, the flaming thatch of hair were charged with energy and power: the same latent power, I thought, that I had already seen on the handball court, lashing out from those long-boned arms to propel a ball like a bullet.

It was after our fifth or sixth game that he asked me to come home with him. And at first I hesitated.

"My wife's a real cook," he smiled. "It will be a good change for you after all those hotels and restaurants."

So I went with him: not north from the Y, as I had always gone before, but south, into terra incognita, through the deep twisting streets of the native city. His mission house was in the very heart of a slum, a nondescript box of a place that might once have been a warehouse, shouldered in by a dismal warren of tenements. But once inside, we were in another world. There was a neat, almost cheerful chapel. There were rest rooms, game rooms, a library, a nursery; even a small dispensary.

"You're not a doctor too?" I asked him.

"No, not an M.D.," he said. "But in this sort of work you have to be a little of everything. And my wife is a nurse."

We went upstairs to their living quarters. Eleanor Bickel greeted us at the door. And it is as she was then I still remember her best, rather than as the other older Eleanor of later years. What I saw first was her smile: the simplest, most natural, most warming smile I have yet to see on the face of a human being. For a moment, too, she seemed very small, but then I realized that this was only because of the tallness of her husband. Pretty? I'm not sure. To this day I'm not sure. Dressed up—made up—she might have been stunning; I never saw her that way. Her hair was dark brown then, her skin smooth and clear. I remember the trim figure, the light step, the firm touch of her hand. I remember the smile. . . .

"I hope you beat him, Mr. Knight," she greeted me. "He's getting awfully vain about his handball."

"Next time," I promised her.

"Yes, see to it, please. Next time."

Back then in '37 there were only the two of them —Jeanie was not born until a year later—but even so, it was not merely two rooms they lived in. It was a home. The furniture was worn but comfortable. There were chintz curtains on the windows and woven mats on the floor. There were books, a bit of china, a bit of silver, in one corner a sewing machine, in another a small portable organ. There was a decanter of sherry, a quick grace, a plain but excellent meal, served with less ado than most women would make over a cup of coffee.

Dinner over, Bickel produced two cigars and his wife went to the organ. I expected hymns, of course, but what came out was *The Blue Danube*, César Franck, the songs from *Show Boat*, finally a Chopstickesque Chinese tune that ended in great one-fingered pounding and waves of laughter.

"Eleanor's the talent in the family," Bickel explained. "Missy Cook, Missy Nurse, Missy Music. I'm just Missa Gab, and they run from me."

Later we talked: about nothing much, I suppose, and a little of everything. Me and my work. Them and their work. Hitler's plans, Japan's plans, the cost of food, the bad bus service, Bickel's project of a small children's playground in a vacant lot down the street. And, of course, of China. Inevitably, China. And when at last I left I told them—truthfully—that it had been the best evening of my year in Peiping.

"You must come again," they said.

And I did. Often.

As Bickel had said, it was a good change for me. From the scurrying around. From the calls and interviews, the big brass and little brass, the getting-it-first and filing-it-first. From nights at bars and nights at poker tables. From the loneliness of a hotel room. . . . But there was more to it than that. For I soon realized that through their eyes, and with their help, I was becoming acquainted with a whole new world: a world immeasurably remote from officialdom and conferences and press releases and embassy receptions; of slums and people and poverty; of hunger and hope; the vast swarming underside of the city's life that was the true, the immemorial China. For the first time, I began really to learn the language. For the first time, I talked not only with administrators and directors, but with grocers, carpenters, mailmen, pipefitters, laundrymen. Through the rooms and hallways of the Bickels' obscure mission flowed the very lifeblood of a country; and there I watched it, touched it, began at last to understand it.

"Off to your sky-pilots?" someone would ask, when I begged off the poker game at the Press Club.

"Off to my China-pilots," I'd answer.

And it was true. That was what they became.

In the process, of course, I grew to know the Bickels themselves. At that time they had been in China for five years: first in Canton, then in an up-river town on the Yangtse, and now, for the past eighteen months, in Peiping. His society was a small and comparatively new one, with only a dozen-odd representatives in the whole of the country, and the essence of his job was to set up a mission, establish it firmly, train Chinese assistants to take over, and then move on to a new field. In that spring of 1937, he judged that by fall he would be ready to leave Peiping.

They both came from Nebraska and had met while they were students at the university at Lincoln. This surprised me, I remember, for I knew that no state colleges had divinity schools; but Bickel explained that back then he had not yet even thought of the ministry and was studying for a degree in scientific agriculture.

It had been a radical switch, hadn't it?

Yes, it had been radical, he agreed. But he didn't elaborate. It was not until years after that I learned what it had been that made him change his plans —and his life.

At any rate, he had left the university halfway through his third term and entered a small seminary in western Missouri. Three years later he was ordained a minister and married Eleanor, and soon after they had left for China.

Why China?

He smiled. "Why are *you* in China?" he asked.

"Because my syndicate sent me."

"All right then. My society sent *me*."

"But that's not all of it."

"No," he conceded, "that's not all of it."

Over the years, I came to know John Bickel so well that it is hard for me to go back and recapture my exact impressions of him during those first days of our friendship. As I daresay I have indicated, I am not, in any formal sense, a religious man. Since childhood, my official contact with clergymen had been limited to weddings and funerals, with an occasional interview thrown in, and of personal relationship I had had none at all. As for missionaries, I was possessed of all the usual prejudices, plus some private ones of my own.

Bickel, however, fitted none of them. He was a reflective and reticent man. There was no pious cant in him; not the faintest tinge of the evangelist, the tubthumper, the naive fundamentalist soul-saver. And he was, I soon discovered, widely and deeply read. On the shelves in his rooms were books not only of religion but of history, biography, politics, economics —and, most interesting of all to me, an extensive collection of oriental theology and philosophy. "I am a Christian," he said to me once, "but I have come to live among Buddhists, Confucianists, Shintoists, Taoists. If I have something to teach them, perhaps they too have something to teach me."

I don't mean to give the impression that he was anything of a recluse, a scholar rather than a preacher. He preached, all right. In the little chapel in that Peiping mission house he preached with all his heart and all his soul and all his might—strongly but gently, deeply but simply—and when the preaching was over he went out among his people, to work with them and play with them and live with them.

For that was what he cared most about. People. The poor, the sick, the hungry; the shopkeepers in their stalls; the peddlers in the street, the coolies in the warehouses, the wild boys in the alleyways; the beggars and pickpockets and prostitutes and hashish-sellers of that dismal slum: these were the human fabric of which his life was made. And, whatever the vision of God he held before him, he saw it, I knew, only through them and for them.

If I am giving the impression that John Bickel was a noble man, that is exactly the impression I am trying to give. He didn't need to tell me why he was in China. He was in China because he believed it was there that human need and suffering were greatest.

Soon, of course, they were to become even greater. It was in that same summer of '37 that the Japs moved down from Manchukuo and took Peiping, and from then on, without respite, war gripped the country for eight bloody years. Shortly after it began I was transferred to Shanghai, then to Hong Kong, then for a year to the States. It was not until after Pearl Harbor that I returned to China, going in over The Hump from India to Chungking. And there, among the ruins and craters of Chiang's battered capital, I met the Bickels again.

I have said that John Bickel was reticent. And so,

too, was his wife. They themselves told me little of their life in the five years since I had seen them, but from others who knew them I got at least a suggestion. They had stayed in China, of course: in the very heart of China, at the heart of war; moving with the armies and the refugees, keeping always closest to where men were fighting and dying, to where women and children were sick, starving and homeless. They had set up their mission in huts built with their own hands. In tents. In forests. In caves. For a year their home had been a sampan on the upper Yangtse, which they operated as a floating First Aid Station just behind the front lines. I would hazard a guess that by the time our paths recrossed they had nursed as many sick and wounded, across two thousand miles of battlefields, as any full-scale medical unit in the Chinese Army.

Most remarkable of all: in the midst of it they had had a child. Jeanie. There she was in Chungking, incredible but real: three years old, pink, laughing; as plump and healthy as if she had never been farther from the nursery than an airing in the park.

I remember exactly what I said when I first saw her. I said, "I don't believe it."

And the Bickels laughed.

From then on, while the war lasted, I saw a good deal of them. In their home (a one-room Quonset). In their makeshift mission, in bomb shelters, along the roads and in the villages of the ravaged countryside, wherever the endless bitter struggle was being fought—and endured. As always, my work involved me largely with officialdom—commissioners and ministers, generals and politicians—and it wasn't long before I, like most outsiders on the scene, was thoroughly fed up with the Nationalist Government. The war had to be fought and won. That was the great and obvious necessity, and everything else had to be subordinated to it. But it was impossible to feel anything but disgust for *how* it was being fought; for the black-marketing and bribing, the cynicism and chicanery, the brutality of the soldiers and the callousness of their officers, the lying and thieving and selling-out and double-dealing that were the routine way of life in wartime China. And it was because of this, as well as for more personal reasons, that I sought the Bickels out as often as I could. My hours with them were among the few bright spots in those grim and disenchanting years. Their simple incorruptible humanity was a shining thing in the world of barbarism and misery in which we lived.

At war's end I went again to the States, but this time I didn't lose track of them, and when I returned to China in '47 I found them established—temporarily, as always—in Shanghai. Things were better with them now; at least materially. Their mission house was larger and better equipped than the one in Peiping. Their home, next door, was cheerful and comfortable. For the first time since I had known them they seemed almost a settled family.

Part of it, of course, was Jean. She was eight now; no longer round and babyish, but an elf of a child; slim, quick and captivating, with the deep gray eyes of her father and the soft features of her mother, plus a vivacity and lightness of heart that were uniquely her own. Back there in Peiping she had not yet even existed. Now she was a person, a personality, the very center of the Bickels' cosmos. More than anything in my own life, or all that had happened in the world, she made me aware of the inexorable march of the years.

Time had changed her parents too, to be sure, though physically less than one might have expected. Eleanor, in Peiping, had been half girl, half woman. Now she was all woman: a matron in her middle thirties; a little faded, perhaps, and plumper than she had been, but still full of the warmth and sweetness that I so well remembered. Still with her radiant smile. Even with Jean to take care of, she worked full-time at her nursing, and the dispensary she had set up in a wing of the mission house was a marvel to see. I well knew what she had been through during the war, but it had neither hardened nor dulled her. She was endowed with that supreme feminine ability to take life day by day, as it came, and make the best of it; and day by day, as she had for years, she cared for her husband, her child and her patients. She was a woman doing what she had been born to do: cheerfully, competently, serenely.

While Eleanor had put on weight, John had lost it. His face, once almost florid, was now lean and weathered, and the bones were prominent. There was a slight stoop in his big angular shoulders. But no gray had yet dimmed the bright shock of his hair; and though our handball days were over, one had still only to look at him to feel his latent energy and power. Yet he had changed: far more than Eleanor. And the changes were less outward than inward. He was quieter than before, often almost abstracted, and deeply withdrawn into himself. Also, he spent hours of each day reading: sometimes from the Bible, sometimes from the modern books on his shelves, but increasingly, I noticed, from the works of the Eastern mystics and philosophers. Whether this was merely escape, or some sort of search, I didn't know. But what I did know—what was obvious in all he said and did—was that what he had seen and experienced in those years of war lay heavily on his spirit.

Nor, to be sure, was the China of 1947 anything to gladden it. Scarcely had one war ended than another began—Red against Nationalist, brother against brother—and each week brought new reports from the north of more battles, more killing, more misery. Still worse, perhaps, was the situation in Shanghai itself, where everything continued in the old pattern of corruption and indifference; and presently the poison had seeped through even into the obscure little world of John Bickel's mission. A few months before my return he had discovered that the mission's most generous local supporter, a Chinese Christian merchant whom he had known for years, had become one of the leading opium smugglers in the city. And soon after, his chief assistant, whom he was training to take over the mission, was caught charging dispensary patients for their supposedly free treatments and pocketing the money himself.

Bickel was sick at heart. He had lost two men whom he had loved and trusted. But his grief and anger were not for them as individuals, for how, he asked, could men be condemned for actions that were no more than the accepted norm of their society?

"It's not only they who are at fault," he said. "It's all of us, and the world we've made. We're lost, Frank: that's what it is. Lost in a jungle. Somewhere we've taken the wrong turning, the wrong direction. . . ."

I know he was glad when, presently, he moved on from Shanghai: this time to the town of Sanchow in remote western Honan. And from the subsequent letters I received—one every three or four months— I gathered that he had again attained some peace of mind and spirit. *Life is simpler here,* he wrote. *Closer to the earth. Closer to reality.* And: *The people are poor, they are sick, they are ignorant. But their patience and gentleness are a thing to move the heart.* And: *We now have a mission basketball team (J.B.—coach), and yesterday we beat the h--- out of a team from the next town. . . .* Eleanor, he wrote, was fine and busy in her dispensary. Jeanie was fine and learning to read. For upwards of a year it was in the back of my mind to go to Honan and pay them a visit. But for one reason and another it never materialized.

Then the Reds came. For a few weeks, early in

'49, the Nationalist press was full of "shortening lines" and "successful consolidations" in the west-central provinces, and when they were over, Honan was gone. As far as communication went, Sanchow might have been on another planet. Once again the Bickels were swallowed up in the dark voiceless maw of China.

I was sure, though, that they had stayed on; and that they would continue to stay on as long as they were allowed to. Wherever there was trouble—wherever there was struggle and want and human suffering—that, inevitably, was where they would be; and, after the way they had come through the Japanese War, I was not too worried about them.

Or at least not until later that year: after the Reds had moved down and taken Shanghai. For now there was no longer a battle-line between the coast and Honan; communications were open; I should have heard from them. . . . But I didn't hear. I wrote, and there was no answer. I phoned Bickel's successor in Shanghai, and he said he had written and had no answer. Twice during the months that followed I applied to the Press Commissariat for permission to go to Honan, but both times it was refused.

There was a silence. A void. Nothing.

The refugee train.

Now nothing again.

The street was narrow, and the house fronts seemed to lean out over it. There was a row of shops numbered 217 to 229; then an alley; then a door marked 231. I tried it, found it unlocked, and went in. Following a corridor, I reached a courtyard and came to another door. This one didn't open, and I knocked.

There was no answer, and I knocked once more. Then I heard a sound above me, as of a window opening, but when I looked up I could see no one. I began knocking again, steadily, and this time, after a while, the door opened and a face looked out at me.

"I wish to see Mr. Ling," I said.

The face was blank.

"Mr. Ling Kei-fu," I said. "Formerly of Sanchow, Honan."

The man shook his head. "There is no Mr. Ling Kei-fu. There is only a Mr. Ling Chei-wei, and he—"

"Then I will see him. You will please tell him I am here?"

"I am sorry, but—"

There was another voice from behind him. "Let the gentleman in, Fung."

The servant opened the door, revealing a dim hallway and a flight of steps. Halfway up the steps a figure in a long house coat stood looking down at me.

"Yes?" he asked.

"I am looking for Mr. Ling Kei-fu," I said. "if you are his brother I should like to speak to you."

"Who are you?"

"My name is Knight. Your brother doesn't know me, but we have mutual friends."

The man was silent for a moment. Then he said, "Come with me."

He went up the steps, and I followed him. On the first landing he opened a door and led me into a softly lit, low-ceilinged room. There was an abundance of furniture, rich hangings, much red and black lacquer, many vases and figurines. When he had closed the door he turned, and I saw that he was a man of perhaps fifty; big for a Chinese, broad and stout, with a round bland face and expressionless eyes.

"Sit down, Mr. Knight," he said. "You would like some tea, perhaps?"

"No, thank you," I said.

"You are sure? I would not wish it thought that I was inhospitable—even to an uninvited guest."

"Thanks just the same."

I sat down, and he sat opposite me. He offered me a cigarette from a jade box, and I took one, and he lit one for himself. Exhaling slowly, he looked at me through the smoke.

"There are no longer many Americans in Shanghai," he said.

"No," I said.

"That is perhaps why my servant was surprised. And worried."

"Worried?"

"As I daresay you are aware, Mr. Knight, Americans are not greatly popular with our new regime. It is not good for a Chinese to be known to have associated with them. No offense, you understand." He smiled slightly. "Merely the facts of life, China, 1950."

He drew in on his cigarette. "In any case," he said, "you are here now. And you are, you say, looking for my brother?"

"Yes," I answered. "Is he here?"

"Just why, may I ask, Mr. Knight, do you wish to see him?"

"I have greetings for him, from an old friend."

"What friend?"

"From a Dominican priest, Father Naganyi, whom he knew in Sanchow."

There was a pause.

"Continue, Mr. Knight," he said.

I hesitated.

"I am sure that is not the only reason you are here."

"Also," I said, "I am looking for information."

"What sort of information?"

"I think it would be better if I told that to your brother."

"No," he said, "it is better that you tell me."

Again I hesitated. Then I said: "It is about another missionary whom he knew. Also from Sanchow. A man named Bickel."

"I see." Mr. Ling studied the tip of his cigarette. "And just what information is it that you wish about this man?"

"Where he is. What's happened to him. Why he wasn't on the refugee train from Honan that has just come in."

"I doubt if my brother would know all these things. It is several months now since he left Sanchow."

"He would know *something*."

Mr. Ling stood up, walked slowly to the window and then back again. "And why, Mr. Knight," he asked, "do you wish this information? You are not a member of this Mr. Bickel's society, I gather. You are not a clergyman."

"No," I said.

"Why, then?"

"Because I am his friend. His close friend."

"I see. And, as a close friend, it is very important to you?"

"Yes."

He sat down again, puffed his cigarette and looked at me steadily. "Important enough," he asked, "for you to make it worth my while to help you?"

"Worth your while—how?"

"I am talking simple business, Mr. Knight. You come here. You ask questions. You are an American; the man you inquire about is a missionary; and both Americans and missionaries are enemies of the Chinese people."

"Are you asking me to believe," I said, "that you are a Communist?"

"I am not asking you to believe anything. I am merely stating certain accepted facts. Today, in this country, there are risks involved in dealing with Americans and missionaries. And where there are risks there should be compensation."

I looked back at him.

"What do you want?" I asked.

"I want five hundred American dollars."

"That's fantastic!"

Mr. Ling shrugged. "It is up to you to decide."

For another long moment I stared at him. Then I stood up. "Where is your brother?" I demanded.

"I am afraid—"

"Let me at least see him. Tell him I'm here. He'll talk to me."

"What makes you think that, Mr. Knight?"

"He was Bickel's friend, too. He would want to help him."

"Oh."

"You won't do it?"

He shook his head. "It would do no good."

There was a silence. We watched each other. Then I turned toward the door.

"You say you are not a missionary," he said quietly. "Now I see you are also not a businessman."

"No," I said.

"I had been under the impression that all Americans were one or the other."

"I'm a newspaperman," I said.

"Ah. I see. But newspapers are business, are they not? In your country, very large business. I imagine they can pay well for what they want."

"My newspapers aren't concerned with this. Only myself, as an individual."

"And as an individual it is not worth five hundred dollars to you?"

"No."

"What *is* it worth?"

I was at the door, my hand on the knob. "Nothing," I was about to say—and leave.

But I didn't say it. I didn't say it, because suddenly I knew it wasn't true. God knows I wasn't overburdened with money. And with such as I had I could think of several thousand things I would rather have done than give it to this Mr. Ling. But once I was out of that door, I knew, all hope of learning about the Bickels would be gone. Nothing would remain nothing. The trail would end before it even began.

"What is it worth, Mr. Knight?" repeated the voice behind me.

I turned and went back to him. Opening my wallet, I took out two bills and laid them on a table.

"Only two hundred dollars," he said.

"That's right."

"It is not much."

"Take it or leave it."

He thought it over. Then he picked up the bills and put them in a pocket of his robe.

"Now take me to your brother," I told him.

"My brother is now here," he said.

There was a pause. Reflexively I glanced around. But even as I did so I knew what I would find, and when I looked back at him I was smiling thinly.

"You must forgive my small deception," said Mr. Ling. "In the circumstances it seemed to me discreet." He paused and reached again for the jade box. "Another cigarette?" he asked.

"No, thank you."

"Do sit down."

I remained standing.

"Where are the Bickels?" I asked.

Mr. Ling lit a second cigarette for himself and blew out a cloud of smoke. "As far as I know," he said, "they are still in Sanchow."

"They weren't killed? They weren't harmed?"

"As I have told you, it is now a few months since

I left there. At that time, they had not been harmed."

"But—"

"And to answer your thought," he went on, "I can almost assure you that they have not been harmed since."

It was partly the words, partly the tone. "Just what do you mean by that?" I asked.

He exhaled another cloud. "Before going on, Mr. Knight, " he said, "I should perhaps tell you two things. The first is that, contrary to what you have assumed, your friend is not my friend. The second is that you are not going to like the information you have paid for."

"Go on," I told him.

"Your friend Mr. Bickel," he said, "has become a Communist."

For a long moment I merely stared at him.

"Fantastic!" I said.

"That is one of your favorite words, I perceive." Mr. Ling smiled. "Well, it is an apt one today. Prices, politics, facts, theories—they have all acquired a certain fantastic quality, have they not, Mr. Knight?"

"This thing that you say: what basis have you for it?"

"The basis of knowledge," he answered. "Of what I saw and experienced."

"After the Reds came to Sanchow?"

"Yes, after the Reds came."

"You mean he stayed. He tried to get on with them. What does that mean? You stayed yourself."

"That is right."

"You stayed on as mayor."

"Yes."

"By antagonizing them? By fighting them?"

"I am not a fool, Mr. Knight. Of course I did not fight them—openly. I have, after all, a certain instinct for self-preservation."

"And Bickel: why wouldn't he have the instinct?"

Mr. Ling shook his head. "With Mr. Bickel," he said, "it was a different matter. I pretended to join them. He did join them."

"How do you know? What proof have you?"

"For one thing, Mr. Knight, I have the proof of what he did to *me*."

I waited. He took a final draw on his cigarette and snubbed it out carefully in a porcelain bowl.

"As I have perhaps indicated," he went on, "I am not a rash man. I wished to continue to enjoy life and liberty. I appeared to cooperate with the Communists. But it was only appearance. Privately, I was working against them: at first by such measures as I could take in Sanchow itself; later, when I saw this was fruitless, by planning to escape to a place where I might be of more use. It happens that I was not only mayor, but also a merchant. If I may say so, a rather prosperous merchant. And over many months I was secretly engaged in liquidating my assets—in making myself mobile, so to speak—so that when I left it would not be empty-handed. By the first of this year all arrangements were complete. I was ready to go. And then the missionary, Mr. Bickel, who had somehow learned of my plans, reported them to the Reds. Fortunately I discovered this in time and was able to make my escape. But there was no chance to take anything with me. All was lost. I became not only a hunted man, but an impoverished one."

He paused.

"So now you see," he added, "that your friend could scarcely be called my friend. Indeed, I wonder, in view of the step he has taken, if he would still be yours."

I didn't say anything. I stood looking down at him.

"And, furthermore, you perhaps see why he did not appear on this refugee train of which you speak. I should imagine that he is quite content where he is."

"That's all you know?" I asked.

"Yes," said Mr. Ling, "that is all I know." He stood up. "I am sorry, but I told you it was not much. And that, such as it was, you would not like it."

He smiled a little. "But at least you now have the essentials. And, if it is any comfort to you, I can assure you that the small sum you gave me is in a worthy cause."

I looked at him blankly.

"Thanks to your Mr. Bickel," he said, "I am now bankrupt. . . . Yes, you have probably noticed this room and its furnishings; but they are not mine. They are my brother's. And he is now selling them, one by one, to support his family. . . . As for myself, I have nothing. Merely hopes. Merely plans. That is what I mean by a 'worthy cause,' Mr. Knight. I have certain connections who can help me; who can get me out of Shanghai—to Hong Kong or Formosa. But it requires money. Alas, everything requires money. And that is why I found it necessary to sell, rather than give, you my information."

He cleared his throat delicately.

"It has a rough justice, you see. Your friend betrays me, but you, in turn, make slight restitution. Not much, to be sure. But a little. It will help. And, as I say, the cause is a good one. Here in Shanghai I can do nothing; no more than in Sanchow. But eventually I shall get out. I shall get to Hong Kong, to Formosa, and there there will be much I can do. I do not mean for myself, but for my country; for my government. For my side in the world conflict, which is also—please remember, Mr. Knight—*your* side. . . ."

I was scarcely listening.

"It is ironic, is it not?" he said. "Your friend becomes an enemy, and I, whom you seem to suspect, become a friend." He regarded me quizzically. "You are still doubtful? You are not convinced?"

Again I went to the door. And again he cleared his throat. "If it is proof you require, Mr. Knight, I might possibly, for another, say, one hundred dollars—"

I went out and down the stairs.

I went down the stairs and through the courtyard and into the street. Then I walked the streets. For an hour, and then another, I threaded their tangled web—slowly, aimlessly—through avenues, squares, alleys, footways, farther and deeper into the dark maze of the city.

This was not the old internationalized Shanghai I had known for years: the Shanghai of the Bund, the boulevards, the neon lights, the clubs and hotels and banks and mercantile houses. Nor was it the new superimposed Shanghai of the "liberators," with its barracks and bureaus, canteens and commissariats. This was still another Shanghai; the Shanghai of the millions; the Shanghai of shadow, of filth, of poverty abysmal and eternal. Overhead the sky was cloudless, but no sunlight fell into the twisting lanes. There seemed to be no air at all. Only heat. Only smells. The smells of ginger, garlic, sweat, urine, excrement.

Crowds swarmed everywhere, less like human beings than like vast colonies of insects. In the streets, squatting against the walls, nursing their babies, emptying their bowels, rooting among the garbage. In long rows of rice-straw shacks, a dozen to a room, without bed, table or chair. At the entrance of an alley was an old crippled woman, crawling on hands and knees to make her family's meal of rice gruel in a rusty tin can. A little beyond, a man sprawled on the cobbles, motionless; whether dead or alive no one knew or cared.

"The Chinese," someone has said, "have had five thousand years in which to louse things up, and they haven't wasted a minute of it." . . . Well, here it was. . . . The China I had merely glimpsed from secretariats, from GHQ's, from hotel balconies and train windows. The China in which John Bickel had lived and worked for eighteen years.

I came out on the bank of Soochow Creek. It was so filled with rafts and sampans that it seemed scarcely water at all, but simply a continuation of the mud-and-bamboo slums. The stench that rose from it was almost overpowering. In the few places where the creek's surface showed it glinted with thick greenish scum. Coming to a low ramp along the bank, I sat down and rested. Through the disorder of my thoughts I tried to recall exactly what Ling Kei-fu had said. Every sentence. Every word and intonation. He might have been lying to me, of course; he was obviously a man to whom lying would come easier than truth. But why? What motive would he have had for lying?

I stopped thinking of Ling and thought of John Bickel. Of the changes I had seen in him between Peiping, 1937, and Shanghai, 1947. Of what the war had done to him. Of his disillusionment, his brooding grief. "Somewhere," he had said, "we've taken the wrong turning, the wrong direction. . . ." And now three more years had passed; years even worse than those before.

I had lighted a cigarette, and suddenly a small boy was standing beside me.

"One for me," he begged. "One for me, mister."

I felt in my pocket and brought out a coin.

"Cigarette, too?"

"No," I said, "you're too young."

The boy moved away and I looked after him. I looked at the bare feet, the splintery legs, the old rice bag that was his only clothing, the bare spots on the back of his head where sores had broken through the hair. And then I heard my own voice; my own words. . . . "You're too young." . . . Too young to smoke. Of course. But not too young for rickets, hookworm, trachoma, syphilis. Not too young to beg in the street, to steal, to starve. Here, boy; here's a coin; go buy yourself—what? A cake of soap? The Bill of Rights? The New Testament?

Had something like this, perhaps, happened to John Bickel? Not suddenly—not all at a time, in a single incident—but slowly, relentlessly, over the years. Had he perhaps felt at last the futility of his work, the hopelessness of pitting his tiny armament of good will and good works against such a mountain of disease and hunger, ignorance and misery? What that boy needed—what four hundred million Chinese needed—was food, clothing, shelter, medicines: the bare bones to build a decent and bearable life. The abstractions could come later. God Himself could come later. Was this perhaps the way Bickel had thought, and, so thinking, renounced a faith that had failed for one yet to be tested?

I got up and walked on, and in the next block a car sped past me. It was a limousine, chauffeur-driven, and in the back were two officials in khaki with red stars on their caps. Ten yards farther on there was a patch of mud in the gutter, and in the mud a little girl, sleeping, while flies crept over her pus-filled eyes.

When the Bickels had been in Shanghai, their mission house had been trim and neatly painted, with a large WELCOME sign over the door and flowers in the window boxes. Now it was almost indistinguishable from the drab tenements that surrounded it. Entering, I found myself in a bare foyer, cluttered with cartons and packing cases; and as I looked around a man came down the stairs carrying an armload of hymn books.

"Mr. Jennison?" I asked.

"Yes," he said. And I introduced myself.

I recognized him as one of those who had been at the station the previous day to meet the refugee train: a plump, rather prim-looking man with thinning hair and—for the moment, at least—a harried expression. He had been in charge of the Shanghai mission since the Bickels had left, but, though I had spoken to him now and then on the phone, when I was seeking information about them, I had not until now actually met him.

"Moving?" I asked, as he put the books in a crate.

"I am afraid it is more than that," he said. "We are leaving."

"Leaving Shanghai?"

"Shanghai. China altogether. We received notice yesterday that we must close the mission and be out of the country within ten days." He produced a handkerchief and wiped his forehead. "Several of the other missions in the city have received similar notice. Apparently it has been timed to coincide with the arrival of our people from the interior."

"Oh."

"I believe I saw you yesterday at the station," he said.

"That's right."

"You too were there to meet Mr. Bickel, I imagine? . . . It was most mystifying, was it not? Most upsetting."

"Did you find out anything?" I asked.

Jennison shook his head. "I spoke to the officials,

of course, and also to several of the missionaries. But no one seemed even to have heard of him."

"One man had," I said.

His manner changed abruptly. "Ah? Yes? . . . What did he say? What did you learn?"

I told him: first about the Dominican monk, then about my visit to Ling Kei-fu. "And that's all I know," I concluded. "From there on your guess is as good as mine."

Jennison had listened silently while I spoke. And now he still said nothing, but merely shook his head slowly and stared at the floor.

"Do you believe it?" I asked.

"I don't know what to believe."

"You don't think it's impossible?"

He looked up. "Yes, of course it's impossible! It's utterly—" He stopped and looked at the floor again, and when he went on his voice was different. "This man you saw," he said. "This former mayor. Would he have any reason for making up such a story?"

"I don't know."

He was shaking his head again.

"Meaning you don't think it impossible?"

He started to speak, hesitated, started again. "I do not know Mr. Bickel well," he murmured. "Our posts have always been in different parts of the country, and all I know is that he—"

"Yes?"

"—that he was of a—well—independent turn of mind. And that he was deeply distressed at the state of the world." Jennison paused. His plump face was clouded. "Strange things can happen in China," he said.

I nodded. For no perceptible reason he picked one of the hymn books from the crate, turned its pages slowly, and put it back again.

"It had occurred to me," I said, "that you might be planning to go to Sanchow."

"To Sanchow—yes—I had considered it. On the way from the station yesterday I had almost decided on it, and then when I returned here there was the notice to leave."

"So now you can't go."

He shook his head. "I have already appealed to the authorities. To go to Sanchow. To keep the mission open a little longer. But they refused everything. By the end of next week, they said, I must be on a ship or plane leaving the country." He was looking at me again, and suddenly I saw that he was close to tears. "It is a terrible thing that is happening, Mr. Knight," he said. "The missions closed; the missionaries exiled; centuries of God's work wiped out as if they had never been. . . . I was born in China, you know. My father was here before me. All my life, all my labors, have been here. And now—"

"Yes, I know," I said. Then, after another pause: "I'll have to be going. I'll call you if I learn anything more."

"Yes—thank you. Thank you." His voice was barely audible. "And now it is all gone. Finished. Mr. Bickel is gone. Lost—"

I shook his hand and said goodbye.

"I have been praying for Mr. Bickel," he said. "For his safety. For his soul." He looked up at me, almost hopefully. "Would you care to join me in a prayer for him?"

"I'll pray for him when I get home," I promised, as I went to the door.

That, I think, was a Tuesday. On Wednesday I wrote a piece about the refugee train that was disapproved by the censor. On Thursday I wrote a piece on the public trial of six "deviationist political criminals" that was disapproved by the censor. And Thursday evening I called my friend Song Foi at the *Shanghai Daily News*.

"I'd like to see you," I told him.

"I am afraid it might be—"

"I mean at your home."

There was a brief pause. "When?" he said.

"Later tonight?"

"All right. At eleven."

Song Foi was both a good newspaperman and a good friend, and I had known him since my first year in China, when he had been a stringer for the Associated Press in Peiping. Educated at an American mission school, he spoke English perfectly and had been westernized to the point where no amount of revolutions or "liberations" could change his basic values and ideas. Not that he was in any sense a counter-revolutionary or Kuomintang agent. For one thing, he had a normally healthy concern for his own life and liberty; and for another, even more important, he had long since lost every feeling save that of disgust for the corrupt Nationalist Government. Outwardly—and to an extent, I think, inwardly—he had accepted the new order, in the hope that, whatever its faults, it could not possibly be as bad as the old. He conformed to the required pattern. He watched his step. But he was no "brain-washer." He had kept his balance, his integrity, his individuality, his belief in tolerance above ruthlessness, in human beings above ideologies. China, I had often had occasion to think, could well have used several million more like him.

I reached his house at eleven, and he showed me into a small room and brought a wine bottle and glasses.

"Can we talk?" I asked.

He nodded.

"I want to go to a place called Sanchow," I said. "In Honan Province."

He looked as surprised as is possible for a Chinese. Then he poured out the wine.

"Why?" he asked.

I told the story again, and he listened expressionlessly. "And what do you, wish me to do?" he said when I had finished.

"I want you to get me a travel permit."

He shook his head. "It is impossible. They would not issue it."

"I don't mean the kind that's issued."

"Oh, I see." Song Foi sipped his wine; then he

looked at me. "They are risky, Frank—these forged permits."

"I'll take the risk."

"At the Shanghai stations they are on the watch for them. During the past month several have been picked up and their bearers arrested."

"I won't leave from a Shanghai station," I said. "And not on one of the big trains. You'll drive me out to Wuhsien in your car. There's only one check-post—on the main road—which we can avoid; and from Wuhsien I can go on from one local train to another. Out in the back country no one will know a faked permit from a real one."

Song Foi thought it over. "Even if it works—" he said "—even if you get to this place in Honan, the authorities here are sure to learn that you have gone. When you return, they will call you in and take away your press card, and you will have to leave the country."

"That will happen soon, anyhow," I told him. "And it hardly matters. As it is, I'm no damn use here. I haven't had a story passed in two weeks."

Song Foi rubbed his chin and looked at the wall behind me.

"This missionary—he is a friend, you say?"

"That's right."

"And you wish to see him for purely personal reasons?"

"For purely personal reasons." I smiled a little. "I promise you I won't try to overthrow the government. I won't sing *God Bless America* on street corners."

Song Foi stood up, walked across the room, came back and sat down again. For a moment he regarded me thoughtfully.

"This is important to you, Frank?" he asked.

"Yes," I said, "it's important."

And it was.

Even back then, at the beginning, it was important—it was somehow *necessary*—that I find out what had happened to John Bickel. I lay no claims to prescience. I had, at that time, of course, not the remotest presentiment of the incredible journey that lay ahead, nor of the circumstances that would cause me to pursue it to its end. I was not even sure exactly when, or how, or why, I had reached the decision to go. Part of it, no doubt, was the futility of my life in Shanghai; the need to move, to act, to *do* something—no matter what. Part, too, was my genuine concern for the Bickels. But there was more to it than that. During the course of the journey, as will be seen, I had ample time—and reason—to look deeply into myself, and I think that I slowly came to understand some of the subtler motives that were at work within me. But then, at the start, I did not understand. I knew only that I wanted to go. That there was a need. A compulsion.

A week after my first visit I returned to Song Foi's and received from him a travel permit, complete with my photograph and signature. And three days after that, in the car which was assigned him for his working rounds, he drove me out through the suburbs of Shanghai to the nearby town of Wuhsien.

There were no hitches. We detoured the check-post. The station at Wuhsien was full of travelers and freight-loaders intent on their own affairs; Song Foi bought my ticket; and no one asked to see my papers. When the train came in I shook Song Foi's hand and got aboard. "I'll see you in two weeks," I told him.

But I have not seen him since.

This first train was bound for Nanking. Nanking's station, however, would have been almost as risky as Shanghai's, and, instead of going through, I got off at a midway junction-stop and changed to a secondary line that ran to the northwest, through Kiangsu and Ankwei Provinces. An American train would have made the distance to Sanchow in a long over-night run, but here in the hinterland of China—and with many changes and waits—it took the better part of four days. When it was available, I traveled second class (there was no first), in the interest both of privacy and of getting some sleep. When it was not (which was for the last two days), I moved into third and tried to make myself as inconspicuous as possible among the welter of humanity, livestock and produce that crammed the crate-like cars.

Only twice was my identity questioned in any way. On one occasion a fellow-passenger to whom I had given a cigarette inquired if I were a Russian, and when I answered yes, he let it go at that. On the second, a new conductor coming through the train asked not only for my ticket but my papers. My passport and visa were in order. My travel permit was a masterpiece of the counterfeiter's craft. The only document about which I had any worries was my press card, which identified me (in English) as a representative of the anything-but-communistic Consolidated News Service; but it was highly unlikely, out in the provinces, that anyone would be able to decipher it, and I had already decided how to do the translating, if necessity arose.

The conductor, however, merely glanced at my papers and moved on. The train moved on. It squeaked and rattled and jolted, hour after hour, mile after mile, across Kiangsu and Ankwei and at last through the parched brown hills of Honan. The sun rose, set, rose again. The car reeked of heat and stench. Everything was filmed with layers of dust and soot, and the bare slats of the benches turned to saw-edges under my rump. Whatever the Bickels' estate in their far corner of the earth, I devoutly hoped that it would include a bathtub and a soft mattress.

Sanchow was indistinguishable from a thousand other Chinese towns. The station was as decrepit as the train, the square beyond it unpaved and almost treeless. There were the usual shopfronts, the usual crowds, the usual mud and bamboo houses. The morning sun was hot on the railway platform, and a veil of dust hung in the windless air.

I went into the station and approached the ticket seller. "Where is the Protestant Mission?" I asked.

He looked at me blankly.

"The mission," I repeated. "Christian. The place of the American missionary."

He shook his head, and, as I turned away, stared after me. Others were staring too. A white man was obviously not a common sight in Sanchow.

I went outside, set my bag down and looked around. There were crowds here, and more stares. Selecting a reasonably intelligent-looking man, I stopped him and asked if he knew the Protestant Mission; but he too shook his head and moved on. I tried two or three others with the same result. Whether they didn't know, or were simply leery of talking to a foreigner, I couldn't quite decide.

No sort of transportation was in evidence. Lugging my bag, I started across the square toward a building, somewhat larger than the others, that looked as if it might be a hotel. But halfway there, I was stopped by a small man in a khaki uniform.

"Where are you going?" he asked.

"To the hotel," I told him.

"Why are you in Sanchow?"

"I have come to see Mr. John Bickel, the American missionary."

The man looked at me sharply. Then he looked away. He rubbed a hand thoughtfully over his cheek and ended by picking his nose.

"You will come with me," he said.

I had expected to be picked up and made no objection. He led me across the square, down a rutted street, around a corner, and turned in at a squat brick building. Over the door was the five-starred flag of the People's Republic and, inside, an office, with many men in khaki and blue cotton.

My guide led me to a railing and spoke to a clerk at the desk beyond.

"Your papers?" said the clerk.

"I wish to see the commissar in charge," I told him.

"Your papers, please."

"My papers are in good order. I shall show them to the proper person."

The clerk looked at me, then at the man who had brought me in. Then he got up, went to a corner of the office and spoke to a man who sat alone at a larger desk. After a few moments the second man came back with him to the railing.

"Your papers, please," he said.

"I wish to see the commissar in charge."

"Why do you wish to see him?"

"To show him my papers. To explain why I am here."

Now it was this one's turn to study me. My guess is that he was trying to decide if I was a Russian. Presently, without speaking again, he crossed the office and went out through a rear door. There was a wait of perhaps five minutes. Most of the people in the office were staring at me.

Then the man who had left reappeared and beckoned. Following him, I went down a short corridor and was shown into a second, much smaller office. There was a single desk, two chairs, a filing cabinet, a picture of Mao on the wall. And behind the desk, a slight, youngish-looking Chinese, wearing a khaki tunic and shell-rimmed glasses.

He did not look up as I came in, but continued

reading a document of some sort that lay before him on the desk. I hoped, with considerable fervor, that it was nothing about me from Shanghai.

"My name is Knight," I began, "and I would appreciate—"

Then he looked up.

"Your papers, please," he said.

I took them out and laid them before him, and he picked up the passport. He looked first at the cover, then at the photograph, then at the Chinese visa, then, with slow deliberation, through all the other pages. Next he examined the forged travel permit and finally my press card. I could see his eyes narrow behind his glasses as he tried to decipher the typed English entries.

"Your newspaper?" he asked.

.."*The Daily Worker*," I said. "Of New York."

He nodded slightly and put the card down. "There are not many Communists in your country?" he said.

"No, not many."

"But in time, perhaps, there will be more."

"Yes, in time."

He leaned back a little in his chair and for the first time looked straight at me. "And why have you come to Sanchow?" he asked. "There is not much here of interest to a journalist.'

"I have come to see John Bickel," I said.

"Oh."

"You know Mr. Bickel?"

"Yes, I know him."

"Where will I find him?"

He was silent for a moment. And when he spoke it was not to answer but to ask another question.

"*Why* do you wish to see Mr. Bickel?" he said.

"Because he is a good story."

"A good story?"

"For my country," I said, "an excellent story. He is an American, a missionary, a type who is usually the worst sort of imperialist and reactionary. Yet here is a man who has renounced these things. He has lived among the Chinese people. He has seen the truth. And he has had the courage to embrace the truth. Such a story would make the most effective propaganda for American readers; and I shall appreciate it, Mr.—"

"Tan," he said. "Comrade Tan."

"—and I shall appreciate it, Comrade Tan, if you'll arrange for me to see him."

Again, he didn't answer at once. His expression was thoughtful, and, in spite of his uniform, he looked less like a commissar than, say, a doctor or a schoolteacher. But this was an impression that dissolved whenever he spoke. His voice was flat, precise, almost metallic; not the voice of an individual, but of a functionary. I had heard it a thousand times: in Chinese, in all languages. It was the voice of our century. The voice of bureaucracy.

"You have heard something, then, of this Mr. Bickel?" he said.

"Yes. In Shanghai."

"Just what have you heard?"

"That he has come over to—our side. That he has

helped in many ways. Specifically, by exposing a former Nationalist official."

Comrade Tan nodded.

"It sounded interesting," I said.

"Yes, it was most interesting." Tan paused. "As you say, he was helpful. Almost from the beginning, when Sanchow was liberated, he showed that he wished to cooperate. The other missionary here—a Catholic priest—was very different. He resisted us. He mumbled into his beads. He went on trying to poison the minds of the ignorant and superstitious. But Mr. Bickel came to us. He worked with us in our program of education and reorganization. And when, several months ago, all other missionaries were expelled from this area, he alone was permitted to remain."

"What about this official he exposed?"

"Yes, later there was the matter of the official, and we were most fortunate that Mr. Bickel was still here. This man—his name was Ling—had been the mayor of Sanchow and was a Kuomintang criminal of the worst order. Unfortunately, however, he was also a very clever man. He succeeded in making us believe that he was on our side; we kept him in office; he appeared to be working with us. But all the while, in secret, he was working only for himself and our enemies, and he would have succeeded in everything, had not Mr. Bickel found out and warned us in time."

Tan paused again. "As a result," he went on, "we were able to thwart Ling's criminal plans. He himself managed to escape; but I gather, from your knowledge of the case, that he has since been caught in Shanghai."

"Yes," I said.

"He has been brought to trial and properly dealt with?"

"Yes."

Comrade Tan nodded. His eyes, behind their glasses, were fixed on my face. "We were confident of it," he said. "Spies, saboteurs and traitors do not flourish long in the People's Republic. We have learned how to find them—and deal with them."

There was a silence.

"About Mr. Bickel—" I said.

"Yes?"

"I should like to see him now. Where is his mission?"

"The mission house is in the eastern part of the town. On the Tung-kwan Road. But you will not find Mr. Bickel."

"Not find him? Why?"

"Because he is not in Sanchow."

"He is on a trip, you mean?"

"No, not on a trip. He no longer lives here."

I stared at him.

"He left," Comrade Tan went on, "shortly after the event of which we were just speaking. Some four months ago now, I should say."

"He was sent away?"

"No, he was not sent. He went of his own free will."

"Where?"

"To Ningsia."

"Ningsia?"

"You do not know it, perhaps? It is the capital of the province of the same name. To the northwest of here, near the border of Mongolia."

For the playing of my role, thus far, I had followed a carefully thought-out pattern of word and action. Now, in an instant, the pattern was gone, and, through my surprise and confusion, I groped for another.

"But why?" I said. "If he could stay here—if he was all right here—"

"I believe he felt," said Tan, "that he could be of more service in a place like Ningsia. It is close to the frontier—a crude place—with few facilities for education or health." He paused. "And also, there were certain events here—certain difficulties, shall we say? —that made him feel it best to move on."

"What kind of difficulties?"

"With the people here. After this Ling had left— and he stayed on."

"I thought you wanted him to stay."

"The government, yes: we were quite willing. But with the townspeople it was not quite the same. With the liberation of China, of course, missionaries no longer have their old hold on the masses. There were those here in Sanchow who perhaps did not know all that Mr. Bickel had done; who believed we were too tolerant of him and wanted him gone. Finally there were certain—disturbances—in which they made their feelings clear."

"What did they do?"

"There were—as I say—disturbances. Certain unpleasant incidents." Comrade Tan was obviously not going to elaborate. "And, as a result," he said, "Mr. Bickel left."

"It was his own decision to leave?"

"Yes."

"And to go to Ningsia?"

"Yes."

I stood up and paced slowly across the room. Tan watched me.

"If there is nothing further, Mr. Knight—" he said.

I turned back to him. "How far is it to Ningsia?" I asked.

"About twelve hundred li, I should say. In a direct line. But there is of course no railway, and—"

"What's the best way for me to get there?"

"For *you*, Mr. Knight?"

"Yes, for me."

"I am afraid there is no way."

"What do you mean?"

He indicated my papers, which still lay on his desk. "Your travel permit specifies only from Shanghai to Sanchow and return."

"But can't you—"

"No, I am sorry." Tan, too, stood up. "Any extension must come from the issuing authority."

"There must be some way—"

"The one possibility is for me to send a wire for you to Shanghai." He looked at me questioningly. "No? You do not wish that, I gather? You have thought better of Ningsia?"

I nodded slowly.

"That is sensible. Even if permission were granted, I should not think it worth your while to go traveling over half of China after one insignificant missionary."

He picked up my papers, stamped them and handed them back to me. "I am sorry your trip was fruitless," he said. "The eastbound train leaves at six tomorrow morning, and since your business here is finished, I must request that you be aboard."

He pressed a buzzer on the desk, and the clerk who had brought me in reappeared. "Mr. Knight will stay overnight at the hotel," Tan told him. "You will see that two men escort him."

The hotel room was a bare cubicle of board and plaster. There was a cot, a chair, a few hooks, a chest of drawers, and, on the chest, a pitcher and basin. My bag lay on the cot, and, taking out my toilet kit, I washed and shaved.

Then I looked from the window. Outside were the square, the crowds, dust, and, directly below me, at the hotel entrance, one of the two policemen who had brought me from the commissariat. The other, I knew, was somewhere around behind.

One thought scratched and gnawed. Had Comrade Tan, on his own, sent a wire to Shanghai inquiring about me? Half the time, during the interview, he had seemed to accept me at my face value. The other half, he had seemed suspicious; but how much of it was specifically of me, and how much simply the natural climate of his job, I didn't know. In any case, it probably made little difference. If he had wired, I would be sent back to Shanghai and then deported. If he hadn't, I was being sent back anyhow—and the deportation would come soon.

I sat down on the cot.

Ningsia, I thought. . . . Why Ningsia?

"I believe he felt," Tan had said, "that he could be of more service in such a place." But why, specifically, *that* place? What had drawn him there—to a place called Ningsia—rather than to any of a thousand other places?

I took a map from my bag and spread it open There was Honan. Sanchow. The hatched line of the railway snaking in from the east. Beyond Sanchow the line continued for perhaps fifty miles and ended at the border of Shensi Province. As Tan had said, there was no railway to Ningsia.

My finger moved on. Across Shensi. Across Kansu. . . . Twelve hundred li. That was four hundred miles. . . . To Ningsia. The town was in the nearest part of the huge province: on the Yellow River, close by the Great Wall. Beyond it the map was almost blank, a sweep of emptiness stretching out into Mongolia and the Gobi Desert.

Why Ningsia?

And why, for that matter, had he left Sanchow?

"Certain incidents," Tan had said. "Disturbances," he had said. It was an answer that was no answer.

I got up, left the room and went downstairs. At the hotel entrance I nodded to the policeman and walked on across the square. He made no effort to stop me, but when presently I looked back I saw that he was following at a distance of a few yards.

I headed east. For perhaps ten minutes I threaded the rutted streets between the mud and bamboo houses, and then I stopped and waited for my shadow.

"Where is the Tung-kwan Road?" I asked him.

He pointed ahead, and we moved on, coming soon to a thoroughfare, broader than the others, that seemed to lead straight on to the east, out of the town.

"Where is the mission that belonged to the American?"

He pointed again, and we followed the road. By now we had reached the outskirts of the town; there were fewer people about, and such as there were were mostly children playing. Or at least they were playing until they saw me, and then they stopped and stared and followed us.

"It is a Whitey," they said.

"A Longnose."

"A new Longnose to take the place of the other."

We passed a market, a vacant lot, a cluster of huts; and then ahead, to the right, was a low wall and, behind it, a rambling two-storey building of tile and stucco. I knew without asking that this was it, and when I came to a gate in the wall I turned in and walked up a gravel path. There had been lawns, I saw, on either side of it, but now they were brown and almost bare, and the walls of the building, ahead, were chipped and stained. A sign at the main doorway proclaimed that it was now a school; but it was obviously not in session, and the only people about were the policeman, myself and the children who had followed us.

I looked around at the children. "Do you go to school here?" I asked.

They didn't answer.

"Did you come here when it was the mission house? Did you know Mr. Bickel?"

Still no answer. The children stared at me and then at the policeman. The policeman gestured at them, and they ran away.

The door was open and I went in. I passed through a hall, a classroom, a second classroom, sparsely furnished with long benches and trestle tables. On the walls were tinted pictures of Mao and Chu Te, Lenin and Stalin. I walked slowly, searching for some relict of the Bickels' tenure; but I saw nothing. In a hall beyond the second classroom a flight of stairs led up to what I guessed must once have been their living quarters. But at the head of the stairs was a door, and the door was locked.

The policeman followed me leisurely, showing no interest in what I was doing. Apparently he had been told to let me do what I liked, provided I didn't try to elude him.

There were more classrooms, then a back door; and

I went out. Here, to the rear of the building, was another path, more withered grass, a few dusty trees and shrubs. Under one of the trees a small wooden slab stood upright in the grass, and I went over and looked at it. There was lettering carved on it, on one side in Chinese, on the other in English. It read:

JEAN BICKEL
Sept. 3, 1938
Feb. 20, 1950

SEVEN

To dispose first of the geography:

The next morning I boarded the eastbound train, as ordered, rode on it for forty miles, and got off at a town called Loyang. I spent a day there, three days cutting back to Chengfu, on the Yellow River, and a week in Chengfu. And on an early July morning, sixteen days after leaving Shanghai, I stepped onto a river-boat, bound upstream through the Northwest Provinces to Ningsia.

There was more to it than that, of course. Much more. On the train I spent two hours locked in what passed for the men's room, laboriously altering my travel permit. At Loyang there were more policemen, more commissars, more questions and counter-questions; but luckily no one bothered sending a wire to Sanchow or Shanghai, and in the end I was declared free to go on. The truck to Chengfu, on which I bought tailboard space, spent a third of the trip being towed by a team of bullocks and another third under repair at a roadside blacksmith shop. In Chengfu, of course, there were again police, commissars, questions—and I must have been a more talented forger than I had realized, for again I was passed. On my third day there I found a trader whose boat was soon to leave for the northwest river ports. On the fourth day we agreed on my passage fare. And on the fifth the fare doubled.

All this, however, was of no importance. It would have been of importance only if I had had to turn back; and though occasionally it was a close thing, this didn't happen. As had been the case in Shanghai, I recall no hesitation or self-questioning about going on. Even more than before, I knew that I *must* go on —as long as I could. A return to Shanghai would have meant even worse than boredom and futility, for I would almost certainly be called to account for my actions and summarily thrown out of the country. Also, the shocking knowledge of Jean's death and the subsequent disappearance of her parents, had made me more than ever concerned for them. Everything about the Bickels was now fogged by tragedy and mystery, and if it was in any way possible I had to get to the core of it. As a newspaperman. As a friend. As a human being.

One thing was lucky, and that was that I had the money to go on. Communist-run banks, I had discovered, have an abrupt and disconcerting way of freezing foreigners' accounts, and I had long since taken to carrying my funds around with me in a money belt. They added up to no great sum, to be sure, but neither did expenses in China's interior. As long as the police kept hands off, I could keep going.

And now, incredibly, there I was: a passenger on the trading boat of one Che Pe-wong, creeping up the roiled muddy channel of the Yellow River.

The first day we made ninety li (roughly thirty miles); the second day seventy-five. Perhaps half the time was spent actually under way, the other half loading cargo at riverbank towns. The third day we had engine trouble and laid over for twenty-four hours at a place called Kichong. At the landings I kept out of sight as much as possible and successfully avoided further questioning by officials.

For the first part of the journey our course lay due north. The heat was intense, the sun malignant, and the current dwindled until the river seemed almost stagnant. But each evening a slight wind came up, blowing low and steady from the west. During the fourth and fifth days we passed two more towns—or, rather, villages: mere huddles on the riverbank, tenanted by barefoot coolies and bullock carts. We were now on the border of Shensi, where the Communist conquest began, but I saw no commissars, no khaki uniforms, no five-starred flags. This was no more Red China than it was Nationalist or Manchu or Sung or Ming China. It was China, period—unchanged for five thousand years.

On the sixth day there was more engine trouble, and we spent the night on a mudbank. On the seventh we were going again, after a fashion, and made forty-eight li. Towns and villages were gone now; the banks no longer green but yellow-brown, like the water. There were no trees. No cultivation. Only bare earth, bare sky, burning sun. And at night the low wind from the west. At last, on the twelfth day, we entered the Great Bend of the Yellow River, and our course veered to the west. We were now in the far north of China, but the heat, if anything, had grown more intense. The river was empty; the land empty. Even in midstream the air was heavy with dust, filling eyes, ears and nose.

Time crept like the yellow current. I had nothing to do, nor even to read. I have called our craft a river-boat, but it was actually nothing more than a motorized sampan, and twenty paces on the cluttered deck took one from bow to stern. Even conversation with the crew was almost impossible, for my Chinese was strictly of the coastal-city variety and I could understand scarcely a word of their back-country dialects. I took to sleeping through the heat of the day, roused myself toward sunset, and spent long hours at night sitting alone in the cooling wind on the foredeck.

Not once did it rain. Not a cloud ever flecked the sky. The stars shone, high and brilliant, and beneath them the wind flowed out of the miles and the night. In the darkness my thoughts moved forward: up the empty river, across the empty land, to the remote town of Ningsia, a speck in the continental ocean. Then they moved back: to another speck, to San- chow, to a dusty yard, to a wooden slab under a tree. . . .

What had happened? How had it happened? Most likely, of course, it had been disease. China was so full of diseases, named and unnamed, that no medical dictionary could keep pace with them. Or had it been an accident? China was that, too: one gigantic never- ending accident. Only one thing appeared obvious: that Jean's death and the Bickels' leaving had been, in part at least, cause and effect. No one could have gone on living with his only child's grave in his own backyard. John Bickel least of all, because he felt things more deeply, and took them harder, than other men.

I had not always known that. In the beginning he had seemed to me too balanced and controlled, too wholly devoted to the service of others, to be vio- lently affected by purely personal emotion. It was not until I had known him for several years that I had my first glimpse of the dark turbulence within him—and learned of the weight of grief and guilt that he carried in his heart.

It had been during the war days, near Chungking, when I had visited the Bickels on their sampan on the Yangtse; and while I was with them word came that a village a few miles downstream had been the scene of a quick and bitter battle, and that the Chinese had succeeded in taking it from the Japs. A battle, of course, meant casualties, and casualties meant that the Bickels must go to them. Within two hours we were there, and, leaving Eleanor and their Chinese assistant to look after the wounded along the waterfront, Bickel and I climbed up the bank to the village proper.

It was a shambles. Almost every house was either afire or already a heap of black rubble, and the dead and dying lay sprawled among them. They were not only the soldiers of both sides, but the villagers as well: old men, old women, mothers, children. There was no order of any kind. No medical unit had arrived. The only activity was the scurrying about of the unhurt soldiers and villagers, busy rifling the bodies of those who had fallen.

In the center of the main street was what had once been a baby, flattened into the dirt as if by a steamroller. Farther on, a severed head lay open-eyed in the gutter. I stopped and was sick against a wall. Bickel moved on, saying nothing, his face bloodless and expressionless.

Then we heard a scream and, rounding the ruin of a house, came to a small filth-littered compound. There were more dead here, more wounded, and in the center of the compound three soldiers and a woman. The woman was lying on the ground, almost naked, with one of the men holding her hands and another her feet. Her body was streaked with blood, and where her right breast had been was a raw red disc of flesh and tissue. The third soldier was standing over her with a bayonet, and, as we approached, he flicked it at the nipple of her other breast.

We stopped. When he spoke, Bickel's voice was very low.

"Let her go," he said.

The soldiers looked up but did not move. "She is a whore," said one. "She lived with the Japs."

"Whatever she was, let her go."

"So you can lay her, Longnose?" The speaker grinned. "Not this one. When we are through with this one even the Japs won't want her."

The soldiers turned away. The one with the bayonet bent lower, and again a sound came from the woman. This time it was not a scream, however, but a low trembling moan.

Then Bickel moved. It was not the movement of a man, but of an animal—a charging bull. In one instant he was standing beside me: silent, motionless. In the next he had already reached the bending man. He did not hit him. He did not shove him. He seemed simply to hurl him. Steel clanked against a wall; a body thudded on the earth; and then Bickel was standing over the body, picking it up, holding it out before him with both hands gripped at the throat. It had taken me that long to move an inch. I looked at the other two soldiers, but they merely got to their feet and stood rooted with astonishment. Bickel ignored them. His eyes were glazed, his face frozen, his hair a wild thatch of flame above them. He held the third man before him—held him at the throat—raised him—raised him until the feet left the ground and the body hung limp, dangling. His hands were as white and huge as those of a marble statue.

Then a tremor went through him. The hands opened and the man slumped to the ground. Bickel seemed to sway a little, and his eyes were closed.

"Not again," he whispered. "God of mercy, not again. . . ."

The other two soldiers simply stared at him. Then, scuttling like beetles, they went to their companion, picked him up and carried him quickly from the compound. The bayonet still lay in the dust by the wall. I went to the woman and bent over her, but she was dead.

When I looked up, Bickel was standing motionless, his hands covering his face. And he did not lower them as I came up beside him.

"What would you have done?" he murmured slowly, tonelessly. But he was not speaking to me. ". . . Christ, sweet Savior," he said "—what would *You* have done?"

It had been that night, back on the sampan, that he told me he had once killed a man.

I looked at him incredulously.

"It was because I killed a man, Frank," he went on, "that I became a minister of God."

And then, for the first time, I heard the story.

It had been back in Nebraska, at the university.

And he had been on the football team. "It was my sophomore year," he said, "and not many sophomores made the varsity team. But to be honest about it, I was pretty good. Even then, I weighed over two hundred; I was six-foot-three; my hands were big and"—he looked down at them—"powerful. But that wasn't the main thing. There were plenty of big strong boys out there in the tall corn, but that didn't make them football players. The main thing—what made me different from them—was that I *wanted* to play. I don't mean just in my head: reasonably, consciously. I mean deep inside me. When I pulled on my cleats and helmet, when I stepped out on the field, I became a different person. Something happened to me. It wasn't the usual sort of thing that would affect a boy: the desire to win, to excel; the stimulation of a crowd. It was something deeper than that. Something dark. Something hidden."

I remember he paused there. I remember he looked down again at his hands.

"Anyhow," he said, "I made the team. I played end and was rated the best tackler on the squad. Not that I was any star, mind you. Our star player was our tailback, a Negro from Chicago named Vic Simmons, a wonderful boy and one of my best friends. No one could stop him. No one even came close until along about midseason, and then it wasn't football but race prejudice. We had a game coming up with one of the big southern colleges, down in their territory, and a few days before it our athletic association got a long weaseling letter from them suggesting that it might be the diplomatic thing if Simmons were left at home. We wouldn't have any part of it, of course. Every man on the squad said he'd refuse to go if Vic couldn't go too, and we sent them a wire telling them so. The next day a wire came back, saying all right—if we felt that strongly about it, Simmons could play."

Bickel paused again, his head still lowered. I had the feeling that this was a story he had told to very few people.

"Well," he said, "we went down. We played the game. And as it turned out, most of the southerners played it fair and decent. There was one who didn't, though—their fullback and line-backer—a big bruising hard-faced hillbilly, the sort that down there they call a wool-hat. From the start it was obvious that he was out to get Vic, and though we did everything we could to prevent it, finally he did. Vic came through the line with the ball, and there was a pile-up; and I was in it and this wool-hat was in it; and then I heard the wool-hat say, 'All right, you nigger bastard,' and when we unscrambled there was Vic with a broken jaw.

"The officials hadn't seen it. They couldn't do anything. But I'd seen it—I'd heard it—and I knew exactly what had to be done. My teammates were hot and angry, but I wasn't hot at all. I was cold. Cold as iron. Cold as stone. And I waited my chance. I didn't get it right away. The wool-hat was the fullback, a line-rusher, and didn't come around end. But then at last—just once—he did. He started through center, hit some sort of pile-up and suddenly veered over toward me. And I hit him. I didn't hit him low, as you're supposed to, but high, with both hands around the neck. I hit him and held him and gave just one jerk, and I heard the bone snap as he went down, and an hour later he was dead. No one on the field had touched him except me."

There was a silence.

"It was an accident," I said.

Bickel shook his head. "No, it was no accident. Everyone said it was, of course; but I knew better."

The next day he had turned in his uniform and a few weeks later left the university. All that winter he had stayed on his parents' farm: keeping to himself, tramping through the snow, groping through the darkness of his thoughts. And when spring came he had entered the United Missions Theological College in Sedalia, Missouri.

That terrible day in the Yangtse village was the only time I had ever seen him lose control. In all other circumstances, however evil, however trying, he maintained his outer calm, his devotion to duty, his forgetfulness of self. Only occasionally, when we were alone and his guard was down, did I have a glimpse of the inward man—and of the doubt and distress that tormented him increasingly as the years went by.

"Who am I," he once asked me, "to bring the word of God to others? How can I dare try, after what I myself have done?"

I assumed he was brooding back to that day on the football field. "That's a long time ago, John," I told him.

He shook his head. "I'm not thinking of long ago. I'm thinking of a ruined village. Of a woman—and a soldier—"

"What else could you have done? He wasn't a man. He was a wild animal."

"No," said Bickel. "No, he was a man. That's the terrible thing. He was a man, sick in his soul; a man who needed God's help. And all I could do was return violence for violence, evil for evil."

Sometimes his doubt was focussed on his own self, sometimes on the world around him. I remembered a night in Shanghai, soon after he had learned that his chief sponsor was an opium smuggler and his assistant a thief.

"Do you know what I am?" he had said bitterly. "An anachronism. The true missionaries today don't bring Bibles with them. They bring checkbooks. They bring guns and tanks, bribes and threats, bread and circuses. They bring a billion dollars. Or the Communist Manifesto."

And later:

"China—" he said. "I've been in China for fifteen years, and every one of them has been a year of war. First against the Japs. Now against themselves. But always China at war—China bleeding, dying—the oldest, most peaceable, most civilized country on earth moving always backward, downward, into violence and savagery."

There had been riots in Shanghai, and we were walking the streets among the wounded and the dead. Suddenly he stopped, closed his eyes and faced into the wind, blowing thin and bitter from the north. "Sometimes," he said, "I almost feel that it's hopeless. That I should go from this country. That God has already gone. That there is nothing to be done for China but to leave it to the wolves of Siberia."

. . . Well, I thought: now the wolves had come. The wolves in khaki. The wolves with guns and tanks and posters and manifestos. The new wolves who were worse than the old dying wolves, because they devoured not only men's bodies but their minds and hearts.

And John Bickel had joined them. That was the incredible thing. He had not left, but stayed and joined them. . . . Was it because his faith was gone? Because, now, Jean was gone? Jean, his only child, the vessel of his hope and love. . . . No, I thought. With all his doubt and sorrow—even in the agony that Jean's death must have caused him—it was inconceivable that he could have changed from one man into another. I could believe that he had chosen to stay on; that, with Jean gone, he had moved on, farther, deeper, trying to lose himself and his grief in the vast anonymity of China. But that he had gone under? No. That he had given up? No. I could as well have believed that the earth was flat, or a stone could speak, as that he could have renounced his faith in men and in God.

As I have said, I am not a religious man. I am a child of my own century. When I spoke the name of God it was usually with a "good" before it or a "damn" after it. When I heard it, it was usually in the peroration of a politician's speech. When I thought of it—which was rarely enough—it was as some sort of vast and abstract Darwinian-Einsteinian mechanism, like the mainspring of a cosmic clock. The God of men like John Bickel—a living, inward, personal God—was alien and remote to me; and now and then, as our friendship grew over the years, I had told him that.

"It's true of so many men, Frank," he had said to me, "because it's true of the world we live in. Sometimes I think back to the Middle Ages: to Augustine and Aquinas and the builders of the great cathedrals. God was very close then, and men were conscious of his nearness. Now it is the opposite. He seems remote, unknowable. But is that because He has withdrawn? Or because we have? Isn't perhaps the answer that now he must search for Him all the harder?"

His own search was never-ending. It led him not merely along the conventional paths of Christian theology but deep into the byways of the oriental faiths: into the writings of Lao Tse, Chu Hsi, Samkara, Tsong-kha-pa; into the ancient holy books of China, India and Tibet. It was not, I knew, that he doubted his own religion, but rather that he was trying to strengthen and deepen it. "Yes, we must go forward with the world," he said. "That is what living is. But sometimes we must also go back. These old men of the East knew something that we have forgotten: that all of living is not merely the evidence of our senses; that there is a reality beyond the senses—beyond the mind—beyond perception and measurement. Call it Karma, Nirvana, the Ultimate. Call it God. It is another dimension, and the only key to that dimension is faith."

That last is what I remembered best. Not his words. Not his theology. But that always, from doubt and despair, he had come back in the end to faith.

I remembered the many places in which the Bickels had lived: the frowzy buildings, the tiny rooms, the makeshift furnishings, but always the chintz curtains at the windows, the old organ in a corner—and somewhere, on one wall or another, a certain picture. It was a small picture, a faded print of some forgotten painting, showing the journey of the Magi to Bethlehem, and it had hung on the wall of every Bickel "home" I had ever visited. The manger and Holy Family were not shown. Only the three wise men, a desert and, above the desert, the star, bright and enormous in what the artist had obviously hoped was a portentous sky. It was an altogether undistinguished picture, and I had scarcely noticed it—let alone thought of it—until one night in the mission house in Shanghai. But since that night I had never forgotten it.

I had come into the Bickels' sitting room, thinking

at first that it was empty, but then I saw that John was sitting on the sofa with his back toward me and that he was staring, motionless, at the picture. I was about to speak, but something stopped me, and, instead, I moved up silently and sat beside him. For what seemed a long time we sat there, still silent, watching it. Then he said quietly:

"There it is, Frank. That is faith. That is hope.

"A star shines. A child is born . . ."

Now in the darkness on the empty river I sat thinking of John Bickel. As he had been through the years I had known him. As he would be now, when at last I found him. Jean was gone. His old life was gone. In the two years since I had seen him he must have suffered doubt and despair deeper than any he had known before. What would I find in Ningsia? What would be left to him?

The picture, I thought: that would be left. And with it, his faith. He could no more have lived without faith than without the cells of his body. The faith that he had spent his life bringing to others; that he needed so deeply, so terribly, for himself.

For a week we followed the Great Bend of the Yellow River. First west, then southwest, then south. The boat's engine broke down twice more and was somehow patched together again.

Finally villages reappeared, and we stopped at two of them. They were different from those of the lower river: no longer Chinese but Mongolian. In the evening the wind blew harder than before, and the sun set into a turbulent cauldron of red, yellow and sombre purple. According to the crew, this was caused by sandstorms off to the west of us in the Gobi Desert.

We passed more villages; a few farms and trees. "We will reach Ningsia tomorrow," said the crew.

And three days later we did.

EIGHT

There were mud walls and rutted streets. There were Chinese faces and Mongolian faces. There was a marketplace, with crowds and camels and stenches and stacks of hides, and, adjoining it, an inn that must have dated from the T'ang Dynasty. There was the burning sun and the dust blowing in from the desert.

And of course there was a commissariat.

This time the person across the desk from me was a woman. Khaki-clad, wearing trousers, her hair pulled out of sight under a peaked cap. But still a woman. A card at the corner of the desk proclaimed that she was Liang Ti-ling, Vice-commissar for the Second Provincial District.

"Why is it," she asked me abruptly, "that you are not in Korea?"

"Korea?" I said.

"That is where history is being made; not here. I should think your paper would want you there, to counteract the lies of the capitalist press." She looked up and saw my expression. "You have perhaps not heard about Korea?" she asked.

I shook my head.

"Two weeks ago the People's Republic of the North was attacked without warning by the imperialist armies of the United States. Needless to say, they have been thrown back with crushing defeats." When I still said nothing, she continued: "Your newspaper is the only one in the capitalist world that would give your people the truth of what is happening."

"We—we have—" The words came hard. "There are others covering—"

"Yes, you have other correspondents, I suppose. A paper as great as *The Daily Worker* must have many. I have read recently in *The North China Press* that its circulation is not quite five million."

"Not quite," I agreed.

Comrade Liang nodded. "In any case," she said, "by the time you got to the fighting it would all be over. In one month, the radio has announced, the invaders will be pushed into the sea." She returned her attention to my papers, and apparently was satisfied with them, for when she looked up again her voice was not unfriendly. "Why have you come to Ningsia?" she asked.

"To see the missionary," I said.

It was her turn to look blank.

"The American missionary who lives here."

"There is no missionary here," she said. "The last missionary was sent away more than a year ago."

"But I was told in Sanchow—"

"Sanchow? Do you mean the couple who came from there? The nurse and her assistant?"

"Assistant?"

"Yes. Her husband and assistant." Comrade Liang rose, crossed to a filing cabinet and returned with a card. "Bickel?" she said.

I nodded.

"Bickel, Eleanor: registered nurse," she read. "Bickel, John: orderly, assistant."

"There's nothing about—" I bit off the words.

"About a missionary? No." Liang went on reading. "Arrived Ningsia, third month, fifth day. Papers in order, stamped by Commissariat Sanchow and Commissariat Ningsia. Established clinic-dispensary and operated same until fifth month, twelfth day. Left Ningsia, fifth month—"

She might as well have fired a bullet.

"Left?" I repeated.

"Yes. Left Ningsia, fifth month, fifteenth day." She looked up at me. "It would have been better if you had made inquiry by wire," she said. "It would have saved you much trouble and disappointment."

There was a silence.

"But in Sanchow—" (It was becoming a refrain.)

"In Sanchow you were told they had come here. That is correct; they were here for two months. But they are here no longer."

"Where did they go?"

"I do not know. Their papers were valid for all of the Northwest Provinces, and it was not necessary for them to specify."

"But you must have some—"

"I was not acquainted with them as individuals," she interrupted, "and I know only what appears on the record."

"Were they sent away?"

"No."

"They went of their own volition?"

"Of their own volition."

"For what reason?"

"The record does not say." Liang turned over the card and shrugged. "Perhaps they were dissatisfied," she said. "Or felt that they had accomplished their work."

"And they went back down-river?"

"The record does not say."

"Someone in Ningsia must know."

"You are free to make inquiries," she said.

I did. During the next three days I asked questions everywhere. At the inn, the marketplace, in the stalls of the bazaar, along the riverfront, in the caravan depots that ringed the outskirts of the town. Many knew of the Bickels, either by name or description. "Yes, they were here," I was told. "Yes, they have gone." But *where* they had gone no one could say.

On the evening of the third day I looked up the captain of the boat on which I had come up-river. He would be starting his down-trip, he said, at the end of the week, and I arranged to go with him. Then I returned to the inn, ate a solitary meal and went up to my room. Most of the rooms, I had discovered, had only a pallet on the floor, but this was apparently the de luxe apartment, for it boasted a cot with a straw mattress. I sat on the cot and looked at the wall.

So this was the end, I thought. The hopeless, preposterous end. . . .

It had been preposterous from the beginning, of course. All of it. The idea, in the first place; the scurrying about that led nowhere; the interviews that led nowhere; the abracadabra with press card and travel permit; the trail from Shanghai to Wuhsien to Sanchow to Loyang to Chengfu to Ningsia; from Father Naganyi to Ling Kei-fu to the Reverend Jennison to Song Foi to Commissar Tan to Commissar Liang. It had been like a journey made in a dream, or a trance, and now here I was, suddenly awakened, in a rat trap of a caravanserai at the farthest outpost of inhabited China, while John and Eleanor Bickel, as likely as not, had long since doubled back to the coast. And quite possibly to Shanghai itself.

Well—now it was my turn for doubling back. To Shanghai. To a summons from the Press Bureau and a one-way ticket out of China. To whatever it was that was happening in Korea. If war had begun, I would obviously be thrown out of the country, with or without the excuse of my having used a forged travel permit. End of the trail, Chinese version. End of Bickels. . . .

Forever?

There was no electricity in the inn. The only light came from a tallow lamp on a table beside the cot. Outside it was now full night, and in the darkness I could hear the low humming of the wind.

A while later, there was a soft knock on the door.

"Yes?" I said.

The door opened and a man came in. He was a young man, short and slight of build, dressed in nondescript blue cotton. As he entered, he turned in a peculiar way to close the door behind him, and then I saw that he had only one arm.

"What is it?" I asked.

"You are Mr. Knight?"

"Yes."

"My name is Yeng," he said. "Yeng Chi-san."

He came farther into the room and the lamplight fell on his face. It was not a northern Mongoloid face, but thin, fine-boned, almost delicate, of the sort most often seen among the Chinese of the south. His voice, I noticed, was of the south too: soft and carefully modulated.

"I have heard of you often, Mr. Knight," he said.

"Heard of me? How?"

"From Mr. and Mrs. Bickel."

I stood up. For a long moment, I think, I simply stared at him. Then I crossed to the room's single chair and pulled it up close to the cot.

"Sit down," I told him.

The man called Yeng sat down.

"It is only by a lucky chance," he said, "that I learned who you are. There has been word around Ningsia, of course, that a foreigner is here. Some have said you were a Russian, others an Englishman. But then today I met one of the crew of the boat on which you came up-river, and he told me your name; and I was at once sure that you were the old friend of the Bickels."

"Where are they?" I said.

My visitor waited a moment before answering. "I am not wholly certain," he told me, "but I think they are in a place called Borba."

"Borba?"

"It is a town far to the west. Many hundreds of miles. On the caravan route to Sinkiang and Outer Mongolia."

I looked at him incredulously.

"Why have they gone there?"

"I am not sure that I can tell you that," he answered quietly. "I am not sure that I know myself."

"Tell me what you *do* know."

He nodded. "Yes, I shall tell you. That is why I have come to you."

"You worked for them here?"

"Here—and in Sanchow. I have lived with them for almost a year and a half."

"You come from Sanchow?"

"It is not my home. I have no home. I came there as a soldier in the Nationalist Army."

I eyed him skeptically. "You don't look like a soldier," I said.

"No, I do not look like a soldier. I did not wish to be a soldier. But neither did thousands of others who were with me."

Like all Chinese, he did not tell a story quickly. And I let him tell it his own way. Back in the late thirties, he said, he had been a law student in Canton. But the wars had put an end to that, and for ten years he had lived the life of an army conscript, first in the struggle against the Japanese and later against the Communists. He had been luckier than most. He had not been killed. He had not starved or frozen or died of disease. But in the end, as with all men, fate had caught up with him. In the late winter of 1949 what was left of his unit had been stationed at Sanchow, in western Honan, and when the Reds came down and drove them out he had been hit by mortar fire and left for dead in a roadside ditch. It was there, after two days, that the Bickels had found him. They had carried him to their mission house, amputated his already gangrenous arm and nursed him back to health and strength.

"From the beginning," said Yeng, "they were the kindest and best people I have ever known."

He had stayed with them. He had become their helper—and a Christian. Most Nationalist soldiers caught behind the Communist lines were promptly given a lecture, a change of uniform and an order to about-face; but with his one arm the Red Army had had no use for him, and he had been allowed to remain where he was.

"The Communists didn't close the mission?" I said.

"No."

"They didn't make Mr. Bickel leave?"

"No."

"Because he himself had become a Communist?"

Again Yeng paused before answering. "No, I would not say that he became a Communist," he said. "Certainly not in any political way."

"But he worked with them? Cooperated with them?"

"Yes. Long before the Reds came he had lost faith in the old government. He had seen too much poverty and injustice and misery. He felt that the new government could at least be no worse, and he hoped he might help the people of Sanchow by staying on."

"What about this mayor?"

"Yes, there was the mayor. Ling Kei-fui. As soon as the Nationalists were gone he came out to meet the Communists and welcome them. He convinced them that he was on their side, and they let him remain in office. Then he began secretly going about among the people, telling them that if they did not pay a certain regular sum, above their taxes, their land and possessions would be confiscated; and all the money he collected he kept for himself. Mr. Bickel found out about it just before Ling was ready to escape to Shanghai, and though he himself did escape, the money was saved.

"The people must have been grateful," I said.

"Yes, they were grateful. While they remembered—" Yeng paused again. "But it is hard to believe how short a time they remembered. And how soon the trouble came."

"What sort of trouble?"

He shook his head slowly. "It was a terrible thing," he said. "For ten years I had been in the army and seen much that was terrible; but never anything such as this. Never that men could turn so on one who had helped and loved them."

Yeng stared down at his one hand. When he went on his voice was even lower than before.

"As I have said, the Communists did not close the mission. They did not interfere with it directly or openly. This was partly, of course, because Mr. Bickel had been cooperative; and also because there were no doctors or hospital in Sanchow and they needed his services for the sick. But they did not really want him there. He was a foreigner, an American, a missionary—a symbol of everything they hated and wished to get rid of—and above all, it was an obvious reproach to them that the town should need the help of an outsider. They kept talking of a doctor and nurses who would soon be sent from Peiping, and when these came, I am sure, they were going to make the Bickels leave.

"Meanwhile there was propaganda. You have perhaps noticed, Mr. Knight, that the Communists are good at propaganda. It is that, not their guns, that has made them masters of China. In Sanchow, for many months, they worked to win over the people. Commissars came. New teachers—they call them *kanpu*—came. There were meetings, parades, public trials of the former merchants and landlords. And every day in the marketplace there was a loudspeaker going: with new music, with great promises, with speakers from Peiping and Shanghai. In the speeches they talked often about foreigners, about missionaries, about the spies and saboteurs of the imperialists, and how they must be driven from the country. Once there was the broadcast of a public trial in Tientsin. It was of six priests and nuns who, they said, had killed three hundred children in their mission orphanage.

"You can see, perhaps, how it was with the people.

They were ignorant. They believed all they were told. And then at last certain things happened in Sanchow, and suddenly it was like a madness—like a fire. There was an epidemic of typhoid fever among the children of a certain district, and some were brought to the mission, and the next day three of them died. That night a crowd came. They were wild, howling. Some were drunk. Mr. Bickel tried to talk to them, but they would not listen. They knocked him down and tied him up: they did the same to Mrs. Bickel and me; and then they went through the mission and destroyed everything in it. The furniture, the equipment, the medical supplies. When the trouble started Mr. Bickel had sent their daughter Jean up to her room, where he thought she would be safe; but a crowd of men found her and brought her down. 'You have done your work on our children,' they said. 'Now we will do ours on your child.' Then they took her into the yard, and ten or twelve of them raped her, and the next morning she was dead."

The soft voice stopped. Yeng sat motionless, looking down at his one hand, and the lamplight flickered yellow on his face. After a while I got up, went to the window and stood looking out at the night. There was an empty street, a scattering of lights and, beyond them, darkness. Through the darkness the wind blew low and humming from the west.

At last I turned back to the room.

"Go on," I said.

"A week later," said Yeng, "we left Sanchow. They

could not stay, of course. Mr. Bickel would not even leave the mission to go into the streets. I think—" he paused "—I think the worst thing of all for him was that it had not been in war—by troops, by enemies—but by the townsmen; his own people."

There was another silence. Suddenly, in my thoughts, it was not Sanchow I saw, but another town. A charred town on the Yangtse—a dying woman—the sprawled figure of a soldier. And John Bickel standing beside them, his face bent into his hands. . . .

"Then they came here?" I said.

"Yes."

"Why?"

"I am not sure that I know," said Yeng slowly. "There were certain outward reasons, of course. For one thing, there had been an outbreak of cholera in Ningsia, and they needed anyone with some sort of medical knowledge."

"Good God, he wasn't *still* willing to work with them?"

Yeng shook his head. "I don't know. In a way, yes —he was. He was willing to go where he was needed. . . . But there was more to it than that. . . . During that last week in Sanchow I scarcely saw him at all. He and Mrs. Bickel kept to themselves; and when he was not with her he was alone in his ruined chapel, praying. Perhaps he was asking God what he should do.

"Anyhow—they decided to come here. And I came with them. I would have followed them anywhere on earth. We came by river-boat, as you came, and when we arrived we found a place to live and work."

"A woman at the commissariat read to me from a file," I said. "It didn't refer to him as a missionary."

"No," said Yeng, "he did not come as a missionary."

"They didn't allow him to?"

Yeng shook his head. "It was not that—no. It was his own decision."

"His own—"

"He did not speak about it. But I was there. I saw it happen. From the time we left Sanchow he stopped preaching and counseling and holding services. He was no longer a clergyman."

"What did he do?"

"He helped Mrs. Bickel with her medical work. When he was not doing that, he was alone, reading and praying."

"He still prayed, then?"

"Oh yes. Constantly." Yeng was looking down at his hand again, as if searching for the right words for his thoughts. "But it was different from before," he said. "Before, he had prayed with others. With Mrs. Bickel, myself, the people. Now it was always alone. Often, here in Ningsia, he would get up in the night and go out behind the house, and through the window I could see him kneeling in the darkness, hour after hour."

"Jean's death had affected him so terribly?"

"That was part of it, of course. The expression of his grief." Once more Yeng hesitated. "But there was something besides that," he went on. "Something beyond it. Mrs. Bickel—she was affected too; for months she was almost sick with her grief. But there was—well—a naturalness in her suffering. It was of the heart, and her heart had not changed. She was the same woman as before . . . With him, though—no —he was not the same . . . With him there was a wall, a remoteness. He was here. At least his body was here. But his mind and heart were somewhere else."

"Yet he still worked, you say?"

"Yes, in the dispensary—and sometimes visiting the sick. It was meaningless, though. Nothing seemed to have meaning for him any longer. Or to touch him. It was as if he were no longer living in the present, or even the past. As if he were *waiting* for something—"

"Waiting?"

Yeng seemed about to go on, but stopped; and there was a silence.

"What happened then?" I asked. "Why did they leave here?"

"I do not know," he said.

I looked at him sharply. "What do you mean, you don't know? You were with them, weren't you?"

"Part of the time I was with them. But not always. There was work to be done not only here in Ningsia, but in the villages up and down river, and mostly it was I who went out to them. The last time I went I was away for a week, and when I returned they were gone."

"Without a word?"

"They left an envelope with money and a note. The note said, *Thank you and God bless you*."

"That's all?"

Yeng nodded. "I inquired everywhere," he said. "At the commissariat, in the bazaar, along the riverfront. But no one knew anything. One day they had been here, they all said. And the next they were gone."

"You spoke of this place to the west—"

"Yes. Of Borba."

"Who told you they went there?"

"No one," said Yeng. "No one could tell me anything. But then, only a few weeks ago—more than two months after they had gone—a caravan reached here from Sinkiang, and in a teahouse I met one of the camel drivers. He said that on their way they had passed through this village called Borba and that there he had seen a white man and woman."

"Did he describe them?"

"Not well. He was a stupid man, and, besides, he saw them only at a distance."

"Then it might have been others."

"It is possible. But, in such a place, I do not think it likely. Particularly since one was a woman."

"But why?" I said. "What would they be doing there?" I paused, groping for a way through the confusion of my thoughts. "Isn't it more probable that they went back down-river? To the east? To the coast?"

Yeng shook his head. "No, I do not think so," he answered. "I think they are in Borba."

"Simply because one camel driver—"

"It is only partly because of the camel driver. It is also—"

He hesitated.

"Yes?" I said.

"It is also because I believe that that was where he had to go."

"Had to?"

"Yes. Into the west. Into the desert." Yeng looked at me, and his eyes were dark and steady in the wavering lamplight. "I know now," he said, "that that was what he had been *waiting* for. . . ."

Again I rose and went to the window. I looked out at the darkness. I listened to the wind. When, presently, I looked back at Yeng, he had not moved.

"Why have you come to me?" I asked. "Why have you told me all this?"

"Because I have heard the Bickels speak of you so often," he said. "Because I know you are their friend."

"What do you expect me to do?"

"I am hoping, Mr. Knight, that you will help me to get to them. As I said, they left me some money; but it was not much. They did not have much. Since they left I have been trying to earn enough so that I can follow them. But with one arm it is not easy to find work. With one arm, no caravan will take me unless I pay my way."

I watched him for a moment without speaking. "You are quite certain," I asked, "that you want to do this?"

"I am certain," he said.

"Even though they left you."

"Yes."

"Even though it means going into the desert. Into the unknown. Into—perhaps—nothing."

"Yes."

"Why?" I said.

"Because I love them," Yeng answered. "Because I want to help them."

I came slowly back to the cot and sat down. For a while the only sound in the room was the low hum of the wind.

A week later we left Ningsia in the caravan of a Turki trader, bound west for Sinkiang by way of the southern Gobi.

Yeng had made the arrangements, and with money at hand there had been no difficulties. For one thing, we were lucky in our timing, for it was now full summer and the season of heaviest travel across the plateaus of Central Asia. Every few days long trains of camels, ponies and men were setting out into the wasteland on their interminable journeys—to Sinkiang, Outer Mongolia, Siberia, Turkestan, Tibet— the thin thread of life flowing again through the wild desolate places, as it had in uncounted thousands of summers along the oldest trade-routes on earth. The caravan would provide our ponies, tents and food. All that remained for us to supply were our clothing and personal possessions, and these we picked up in the bazaar of Ningsia. I traded my suitcase for a pair of canvas saddle-bags. I bought khaki trousers and shirts, a pair of Mongolian boots and a cape-with-hood contraption for protection against wind and sand. I would also have liked to acquire sun-glasses, a flashlight and a ration of toilet paper, but I might as well have been looking for a Cadillac convertible.

Momentarily I expected the ax to fall. A wire would arrive at the commissariat; a policeman would move up beside me; I would appear again before Comrade Liang and be packed off in the direction from which I had come. But it didn't happen. Nothing happened. And on the morning of my tenth day in Ningsia, Yeng and I mounted our ponies in a caravan depot on the town's outskirts and headed west into the empty land.

Shanghai, Sanchow, Ningsia. . . . And now Borba. . . . Now the steppes, the deserts, the mountains, and, beyond them, a thousand miles distant in the deep heart of Asia, a tiny settlement, a caravan cross-roads, a place called (for some reason, presumably) Borba. I thought of Henry Stanley doffing his topee: "Dr. Livingstone, I presume?" Of Conrad's Marlowe: "Mr. Kurtz, I presume?" Now it was Frank Knight: "Mr. Bickel, I presume?" There were times when I half smiled. But beneath the smile there was still the question, still the void. Beneath the implau-

sibility and fantasticality and quixotic senseless-
ness of my search, there was still the need, the compulsion, to continue the search.

There were times, to be sure, when I questioned
the sense, even the sanity, of what I was doing. I
might never find the Bickels. If I did find them—
what then? My syndicate didn't know where I was,
and I had no way of letting them know. There were
any number of valid reasons for turning back; but for
each of them there was a stronger deeper reason for
going on. I was not, after all, abandoning my post in
Shanghai, because there was, in effect, no longer a
post to abandon. I was on the margin of an area
which few westerners had ever seen, and, as the
heartland of the new communist world, it might well
produce a truly "big" story. But my strongest motive,
I think, was the simple fact that I had already com-
mitted myself. To have turned back now, empty-
handed and beaten, would have outraged every instinct I possessed, both as a newspaperman and as a
human being. I had to go on. If it was the last thing
I did on earth (and sometimes this seemed not unlikely), I had to learn what had happened to John
and Eleanor Bickel.

And also . . .

Also, there was one further thing of which I had
become increasingly aware as I moved on in my journey. I not only felt the necessity of going on. I
wanted to go on. Where it would end—what I would
find—I didn't know. But what I did know, with absolute certainty, was that, for the time being at least,

I had had all of my old life that I could endure. I don't mean merely the boredom and frustration of that last year in Shanghai. I mean something far more than that. For fifteen years I had been a newspaperman, a correspondent, a hired watcher and recorder of the world's convulsions. I had heard the speakers—and the guns. I had smelled the cordite—and the corpses. I had seen the armies, the mobs, the hounded, the starving, the long rows of kneeling figures with the steel at their necks and their self-dug graves before them. Worst of all, I had known the fear and ignorance, the lust for power, the blindness of heart which had made these things possible. I am a reporter—yes. It is my trade to know and to record. But I am also a man; every man has his point of surfeit; and there, in that summer of 1950, I had reached mine. It was not a soldier's surfeit: of killing, of the fear of death. In a way it was worse. It was the surfeit of the onlooker, the uninvolved, the privileged, the God-player, and it lay like a cold mortmain on my mind and heart.

Now I was in a place called Ningsia. A speck on the map. An outpost. A frontier. To the east was the China I had known, the world I had known—the world of fear and ignorance and hatred and everlasting war—now of yet another war, just beginning, between the two halves of the earth, that might soon grow into the last and greatest of all wars. To the west was the unknown, the open land, silent and empty.

I went west.

On the first day we passed through a scattering of villages and plowed fields. On the second, for several hours, we followed the ancient crumbling spine that forms the farthermost reach of the Great Wall of China. Then village, field and wall alike disappeared, and we moved on between the bare planes of earth and sky. We moved on a hundred li a day; camped, slept, broke camp, moved on again; and we were the only things that lived or moved within the circle of the horizon.

For the first week the earth was mostly brown grassland. Now and then we would cross the bed of a dried-up stream, and once—only once—we came to one with a trickle of water and, beside it, a file of trees, standing gaunt and forlorn against blue distance. Then even the grass was gone. In its place was rock and sand. To the north, a range of wrinkled hills appeared, undulated and vanished. The sun beat down; the wind flowed from the northwest; we moved hunched and plodding into the blowing sand. During the long hours of daylight it was hot almost to burning, but when the sun set it grew suddenly cold, and we slept close to our dung fires under the glittering stars.

The naked loneliness of the land pressed in upon us, and we traveled in almost unbroken silence. It was a silence that might ordinarily have depressed me, but in my present frame of mind I found it deeply welcome. Behind us the sun rose out of a world in torment; ahead, it sank into another world for which the prospects were little better. But here, in the old heart of Asia, the sound and fury of man-made strife were far away. Here in the quiet places, man was no longer the center and focus, prime-mover and destroyer of the earth, but was barely suffered to exist, to crawl painfully against the ground across a gigantic sterile planet of rock and wind. It was good, for however brief a time, to lose all touch with the currents and pressures of living; to move outward in distance and backward in time from the clamor and savagery and frustration of human living. I swayed through the days on the back of a shaggy-haired pony, and my mind breathed in great drafts of stillness and space.

"Very big, China." . . . That was Noel Coward (of all people). . . . We were still in China. For the first two weeks we were still in the province of Ningsia. But we had left the world.

Yeng and I rode in the middle of the caravan: myself usually ahead, he a few paces behind. Like the others, we rode in silence, and even at night, by the cook-fires or in our tent, we spoke very little. We did not speak of the Bickels at all. And after the first few days I found myself scarcely thinking of them. There was nothing left to speak of; nothing left to think. There was only the day's journey, and the next, and the next. There was only wind and sand and sun and bare horizon, and beyond the horizon—whatever we would find.

In a general way I kept track of our progress. Our course was west by slightly north, our average daily march thirty miles, a pace that would bring us to

Borba in a little over a month. Somewhere about the middle of the journey we passed from Ningsia into Sinkiang, and far to the south we had occasional glimpses of the white snowpeaks of the Nan Shan Mountains.

But in all other directions the earth remained flat and empty. Out of this emptiness, every few days, there would arise, like a mirage, a forlorn village or cluster of hide tents, and we would stop briefly, water our animals, and engage in what little trading the place offered. The people here were no longer Chinese, but Mongol: squat and heavy-set, with stolid weathered features and the bowed legs of horsemen. . . . Communist? Nationalist? . . . One might as well have asked if they were Republicans or Democrats. The Chinese in our caravan were obviously as much outlanders to them as I was, and they simply stared at all of us, withdrawn and alien, until we set out on our way again and their village faded in the distance.

July . . . what? I had lost track of the days. Indeed, there were no days, but only light and dark. The sun seemed to mock us: rising behind, moving past, setting ahead. Then the same thing again. And again. It was as if we, not the earth, were moving in a great circle, returning each day to where we had been the day before.

Wind. Sand. The sand blew into eyes, ears, nose, clothing. It grated between the teeth. Above the wind the sky glared like a sheet of brass.

Imperceptibly we were gaining altitude; the nights were colder. But the days were a blue oven. The earth had been burnt to a cinder. Hour after hour I rode with my hood almost covering my face: not only as protection against wind and sand, but to shut out the desolation, the emptiness. The hood was a pocket of refuge against the monstrous emptiness.

One afternoon, suddenly, the wind rose into a storm. The sand battered against us in horizontal waves; soon the whole caravan stopped; men and animals huddled, rump to the blast, waiting it out. It went on for an hour, with a sort of demented violence, as if it were trying to rip the last tatters of flesh from the earth's bare bones. Then, as suddenly as it had come, it was gone. For the first time in days there was no wind at all. When night came there was still no wind. Beyond the tents the earth spread away in frozen stillness. But the sound of the stillness was the sound of the wind.

I thought of the blue miles behind me. Of the world behind me. Of Korea. Of the new war, the next war, the next step in the everlasting war, that, day by day, must be growing, spreading into—what? Perhaps by now it was not only Korea, but China too. Perhaps Russia, Europe, the world. I should have been there: at my phones, at my interviews, at the command posts and secretariats and GHQ's. I should have, but I wasn't, and I thanked God that I wasn't. You will get there in good time, I thought. If not for this war, for the next—or the next. In time for the big bang; for the kill. In time to oil the typewriter for Armageddon and beat the A.P. man to the cable office on Judgment Day.

I thought of the blue miles ahead. Of Borba. The speck in the desert ocean. The reason for its existence, I had learned, was that it marked the junction of two great caravan routes: our own, leading east-west from China to Turkestan, and another, running north-south between Mongolia and Tibet. Some of the other travelers in the caravan had been there before, but they were at best poor tourist agents and I had little idea of what to expect. Presumably the revolution had swept even that far. There would be commissars and *kanpu*, or at least a Red Army garrison. Conceivably there might be trouble. That, however, was a chance I would have to take, and thinking about it was as fruitless as thinking about Korea.

Or about John and Eleanor Bickel.

I thought of the wind, and the wind rose again, and we plodded on. We were sleepwalkers. Sleepriders. The blue miles unrolled in the changeless tapestry of a dream.

Then an apparition appeared: another caravan, moving east. . . . Marco Polo, perhaps? Or a Russian general? Hunters of the desert hare? Or of uranium? . . . All I saw were the flat weathered faces of plainsmen, and from the shouts that came over the intervening ground I learned that we were only three days from Borba.

First Day: By now it was obviously well into August. Arbitrarily I selected a date. As the day broke and I came from my tent, I said, "I christen you August ninth." It gave me quite a godlike feeling.

Second Day: Exercising my temporary prerogative, I designated this also August ninth. (Which, I later discovered, put me only two days off, instead of three.) The world was sand, the world was sun, the world was wind. And that was all it was—until, at last, it was also night. In the darkness beyond the tent flap I could see a kneeling figure. It was Yeng, praying; and though his prayer was silent I knew whom it was for.

Third Day: (August tenth—or eighth.) The land changed at last. There was sparse grass, a thin stream, a stagnant lake. Toward noon we saw dark specks in the sky ahead, but this time they were not blowing sand. They were vultures. And at last, beneath the vultures, appeared men and animals, mud walls, Borba. . . .

It lay dirty, parched and sprawling under the brazen sky. Dust rose in clouds from the narrow streets; the air was filled with nameless stenches; the vultures circled—watching, waiting. But for all its squalor, all its remoteness, the place was vibrant and alive. Long files of camels, ponies and men moved endlessly between the mud walls. Children shouted. Beggars whined. And in the central square swarmed the faces and races of Eurasia: slight, blue-bloused Chinese from the cities to the east; squat Mongols from the steppes; bearded Moslems from Turkestan; Manchus and Kurds; Kirghiz, Tungans, Buriats, Kalmuks, Tibetans; herdsmen and camel-drivers, merchants and lamas; men of all the stocks and tribes of the inland continent, drawn to the only marketplace in a million square miles of empty land. My eyes searched among them for signs of the new order: for khaki tunics and red stars. But I saw none.

What I did see, suddenly and incredibly, was Eleanor Bickel.

ELEVEN

She saw Yeng first. Or at least she recognized him first. We swung down from our ponies and went toward her, and she stopped and stared at him. Then she took his one hand in both of hers.

"Yeng," she murmured. "Dear Yeng—"

Looking past him, she saw me. And I spoke her name. This time she stared longer, her eyes dark-blue and clear and deep, exactly as I remembered them; and this time she said nothing at all, but suddenly turned a little and took a half step toward me. Then she was close against me; her head was bent; the brown and yellow faces of the marketplace flowed by, forgotten, while I held her gently, silently, in my arms.

Yeng got the ponies and came back. Then at last she looked up again. She had not been crying. I had never seen her, nor could I imagine her, crying. But her lips were tight and trembling slightly, and she seemed still unable to speak. She looked at the ponies, again at Yeng, again at me. And I looked back at her. At the blue eyes, the soft oval of her face, the brimmed straw hat, the neat cotton dress. At the basket slung on her arm, for all the world as if she were going around the corner to the A & P.

I think I smiled.

"You—you're marketing," I said inanely.

She nodded.

"We'll help you."

"Oh no. No, thank you; it's all done. And it's so hot. You must be tired—" She was looking at our faces, our clothing, the sand and grime that covered them. "After such a trip—"

I took the basket from her arm.

"We'll go home," she said. "Of course; right now. You both must be—"

"Is that where John is?"

"John?" For an instant—the merest instant—she hesitated. It was almost as if I had spoken a name that was strange to her. "No," she said, "John is away just now."

"Away?"

"In one of the desert villages."

"Will he be back tonight?"

"No, I don't think tonight." There was a brief pause, and she turned to Yeng. "There's the caravan depot across the square," she said. "There are porters there who know where we live. They'll bring your things and Mr. Knight's."

"Yes, my lady."

Yeng started to lead the ponies off, but she called him back. She went close to him and raised her face and kissed him on the cheek. "God bless you, dear Yeng," she said.

"Wouldn't it be simpler," I put in, "if I went to an inn?"

"It would not." She turned quickly. "You're coming right home with me."

"But—"

She was having no buts. "The *serais* are filthy," she said. "Even in our place it's hard to keep clean, and you must be sure to delouse yourself every day."

I smiled. "Is Borba as bad as that?"

"It's nothing to smile at. There have been more than two hundred cases of typhus in the last month."

I stopped smiling and promised to obey instructions. Yeng went off across the square with the ponies. And suddenly we were standing there, the two of us, wordless. We were standing in the marketplace of a town called Borba, with the men of the desert around us, the camels and ponies around us, sky and sand and a thousand miles of emptiness around us, and there she was in the midst of it, with her quiet blue eyes, her white face, her straw hat, her cotton dress— there was Eleanor Bickel, at last before me—alive, palpable, no longer an image but a woman—and yet somehow, suddenly, less real that an image, less plausible than a dream.

Her eyes were searching my face.

"It—it really is you," she murmured. "I can't believe—"

"Nor can I," I said.

"—that in all of China—this way—by accident—"

"It's not accident, Elly."

She started to speak, stopped, stared at me. Again her lips moved, but no words came. Briefly, I told her about my long search. From Shanghai to Sanchow to Ningsia, to Borba. From Father Naganyi to Ling Kei-fu to the two commissars—and at last to Yeng. And she listened quietly, her eyes never leaving my face, and when I had finished she still said nothing, but only raised her hand a little and let it drop, and then at last closed her eyes.

"Oh, Frank," she whispered. "Frank, my dearest—"

Yeng returned, followed by two Mongols with our saddle-bags, and quickly she got hold of herself.

"We'll go home now," she said. "It isn't far."

Turning out of the marketplace, we followed one of the narrow mud-walled streets. Every few steps Eleanor was greeted by passersby, and such curious stares as we encountered were directed only at me. Apparently she and her husband were already accepted fixtures in this remote desert crossroads.

Of course, I thought. It is "home." We are "going home." And then I was thinking back to the other strange and unlikely places that had been "home" to the Bickels over the past fifteen years. The slums of Peiping and Shanghai; the caves and thatch huts of the war years; the Quonset at Chungking and the sampan on the Yangtse; a place called Sanchow, a place called Ningsia. Now a place called Borba. They belonged in one place no more and no less than in another. And as we walked the streets of a trading post in the wastes of Sinkiang, it was again "home" toward which we were going.

We walked almost in silence. Here she was, at last. The long search was over; I had found them; the questions and fears that had plagued me for months past could be answered and resolved. But the questions were too many, the fears too deep and formless, and suddenly, insanely, there seemed nothing to say at all. Constraint held me voiceless. And Eleanor as well. I knew how great was her astonishment at finding me there, and in a whispered word she had told me of her gratitude. Even now she must have been feeling her way, step by step, through the maze of the two years since last we had met. But for her, as for me, the maze was too deep; too dark. There was so much to say, and there was nothing to say. Not so quickly. Not yet. . . .

Then I said:

"Does John go away often?"

"Fairly often," she said.

"How long does he stay?"

"Usually only a few days."

"In these desert villages?"

"Yes, in the villages."

And a little later:

"You're looking fine, Elly."

"So are you," she said.

"I'm looking dirty."

She smiled. "That's something we can take care of."

"Thank God," I said. "My last bath was in Shanghai, two months ago."

We walked in silence again.

John walked beside us. Jean walked beside us.

Then we came to where the Bickels lived.

Outside it was dried mud, the same as all the other houses. But inside, somehow—and miraculously—it was "home." There were a few pieces of western furniture, a shelf of books, string rugs, chintz curtains. On one table was an open sewing basket, on another a rack of pipes. And the old portable organ stood familiarly against a wall.

I don't know why, but I went over and touched it.

"We managed to save it," said Eleanor. "It was broken in Sanchow, but John put it together again."

She spoke without looking at me, and I didn't say anything. Then Yeng and the porters came in, and I paid the porters off, and Eleanor said, "Now I'll show you to your room and heat up some water."

It was less a room than a cubicle. As in the inns at Sanchow and Ningsia, the only furniture was a cot and a chest of drawers. But this cubicle was clean. It had a rug and curtains. And on the wall over the cot was the faded print of the Journey of the Magi that I had seen so often before in so many Bickel "homes."

I was taking off my boots when there was a knock

on the door and a boy came in. He was a Mongolian boy of about eleven or twelve, with black bright eyes and a button nose, and he was half carrying, half dragging a galvanized iron tub.

"I am Khitai," he announced in English.

"Hello, Khitai."

"Now I bring water," he said, and disappeared.

While I undressed, he returned half a dozen times with a steaming pitcher, which he emptied into the tub. And on his last trip he brought soap and a towel.

"My mother asks," he said, "if you need anything else."

"Your mother?"

"Mother Bickel." He looked at me proudly. "I am Khitai Bickel."

"Oh. . . . No thanks, Khitai. I'm all fixed now."

I spent the better part of an hour soaking the dirt and stiffness from my body, then put on my nearest approximation to fresh clothes. By the time I had finished it was growing dark. Going out, I passed through the living room and found Eleanor at an old iron stove in the kitchen.

"Let me help," I said.

"All right," she answered. But she only sat me down and gave me a rolled wad of paper. "Guard duty," she explained. "When you see a cockroach, jump."

I sat watching her, and the stove hummed, and it was the pleasantest sound I had heard in a long time. Eleanor, just as she always had, moved quickly and deftly at her work. Suddenly, happily, it seemed two weeks, rather than two years, since I had last sat in a Bickel kitchen.

Presently the Mongol boy came in, carrying a load of fuel that looked like dried slabs of mud.

"You've met Khitai?" said Eleanor.

"Oh yes. He was my bath steward."

After a few moments the boy went out. Eleanor turned and must have seen the question in my eyes.

"We've adopted him," she said. "Both his parents died last month of typhus."

"He looks like a good boy."

"Yes, he's good. He needed a home so badly." She paused. "And we needed him," she added.

Khitai came and went. Then Yeng appeared, wearing a blue blouse and house slippers, and, without instructions, began lighting the oil lamps and setting the table.

"For four, Yeng," said Eleanor.

"Thank you, my lady. But—"

"For four," she repeated, smiling. "I count four in the family."

When the food was ready she brought it to the table, and we all sat down.

"Yeng, would you—?" she asked.

And Yeng said grace.

Then we ate. The meal—as in all Eleanor's "homes"—was plain but excellent, and after two months of rice and dried camel-meat I was all the guest any hostess could have asked for. At first the talk was casual and desultory: about second helpings, the problems of marketing in Borba, the wind-blisters on Yeng's lips, the workings of my wristwatch (which was obviously the most fascinating object Khitai had ever seen). Then I told Eleanor of a few incidents on the boat- and caravan-trips that I thought might interest or amuse her. But I veered carefully away from the significant incidents—the talk with the commissar in Sanchow, the visit to the mission house, the meeting with Yeng—and she, for her part, neither asked questions nor volunteered any information of her own.

It was not until the meal was almost over that I succeeded in getting her to speak of herself and John, and then it was only about their day-to-day life in Borba. At first they had been very busy, she said; during the height of the typhus epidemic they had taken care of almost a hundred patients. But now it was no longer so bad—at least in the town itself. It had spread to the surrounding villages and nomad camps, and during the past month John had made a weekly round of them.

As he was doing now?

There was a barely perceptible pause before Eleanor answered. Then she said, "Yes, as he's doing now."

"Is there any danger from bandits?"

"Not for us. We've nothing that they could want."

"What about the government?"

"The government?"

"It lets you do your work. It doesn't interfere?"

"Out here the government is far away. There are only troops; a small garrison." Eleanor paused again:

longer than before. "And also—also, you see—John doesn't—he isn't—" She couldn't say it.

"He isn't a missionary any more?" I said.

She looked at Yeng, then suddenly down at her plate. "No," she murmured.

"He's stopped preaching, altogether?"

"Yes."

"And does only medical work?"

"Yes." She didn't raise her eyes. Her hands were motionless on the table. "John isn't as you remember him, Frank," she said. "He's changed. He's different."

We had now finished eating, and before I could speak again she had risen and began clearing the table. The three of us helped her, and, after some argument, I was permitted to dry, while she and Yeng washed, the dishes. When we were through, Yeng excused himself and disappeared. Khitai, who had gone outside briefly, came back, kissed Eleanor good-night and shook my hand gravely.

"You wear the watch on the left hand, sir," he asked, "so it will not be hurt when you strike your enemies?"

"I guess that's one of the reasons," I told him.

He nodded. "That is wise. Very wise. When I am a man and have a watch, I will keep it in my saddle-bag when I ride into battle."

Then he, too, went to his room, and Eleanor and I were left alone in the little parlor. It was night now, and two oil lamps threw a yellow glow on the walls and ceiling. We sat down and I waited for her to speak. But she didn't. And, again, I too was wordless, and for a few moments the only sound was the murmuring of the wind that had risen in the street outside.

Then she said: "This was when John always brought out the cigars. But they're all gone, I'm afraid."

"That isn't gone," I said, pointing.

She looked at the farther wall. "The organ?"

"Yes. Would you play for me?"

"Oh Frank, it's been so long. I don't know if—"

"Just one piece, Elly. Please."

She hesitated. Then she got up, crossed slowly to the organ and sat down at it. Her feet worked the pedals, it gave a tired wheeze, and she laid her hands on the keyboard.

"Some of the keys are broken," she said.

But when the music came out it was low and sweet, seeming to mingle like liquid with the glow of the lamplight. She played a little Chinese piece and then one of her favorites from César Franck, and I sat listening and trying to visualize that battered organ traveling across the miles of Asia on the deck of a river-boat and the swaying back of a camel. Then it was no longer the organ I saw, but Eleanor. On the great river, in the empty wastes—in Sanchow, Ningsia, now in Borba—sitting at the organ with the lamplight on her hands and face. The hands seemed larger than I remembered them; the bones more prominent, the skin reddened and rough. And in her face, too, there was more bone. It was thinner than before—almost as thin as when I had first known her

—but it was no longer the delicate thinness of a young girl. Her eyes, bent to the keyboard, appeared tired and shadowed. . . . Or was that, perhaps, only the lamplight?

When she finished playing she sat silently, and again I could hear the wind in the night beyond the windows.

I got up and went over to her.

"Are you alone much, Elly?" I asked.

"Just now and then," she said. "When John goes off to the villages."

"Do you ever go with him?"

"I used to when we first came here. The last few times he has gone alone."

"How long does he stay?"

"Often just overnight. Sometimes a little longer."

"How long this time?"

"He left four days ago," she said.

I sat down beside her on the organ stool.

"Tell me about it, Elly," I said gently.

She didn't answer.

"About John. You said he's changed. Tell me how."

Another moment passed. She did not look at me.

Then she murmured: "Of course Yeng has told you what happened. Back in Sanchow—"

"Yes."

"It was unbelievable, Frank. Like some sort of hideous dream. I don't know how we lived through it."

I put my hand on hers.

"Sometimes," she said, "I'm not sure that John *did* live through it." She paused. For a moment she closed her eyes. Then she went on: "It was terrible for us both, of course. For weeks after it happened I thought, truly, that I was going out of my mind. All my strength was gone. I wanted to die. Day after day I simply lay on my bed and prayed to God that in exchange for my death He would let Jean live again."

She paused.

"John prayed too," she said. "He prayed almost all the time. . . . But there was a difference. I knew it. I could tell. . . . After a while I found—well—resignation; a sort of peace. But John didn't. For a while I thought that almost anything might happen; that he might break out suddenly into some awful violence. But that didn't happen either. It might almost have been better if it had. Instead, he began to act as if the world no longer existed for him, turning deeper and deeper into himself."

"And he stopped preaching?"

"Yes."

"From the very beginning?"

"In Sanchow there was no one left to preach to. No one would come to the mission. Then when we moved on, he still didn't. . . . He couldn't."

I got up and walked slowly across the room. Eleanor didn't move.

"You should have left," I said.

"Left?"

"After Sanchow. You should have gone to Shanghai—got out of China. It's no good for you any more."

"We talked of leaving. I suggested it. But—"

"But he wouldn't?"

"No."

"Why? . . . Because he'd become a Communist?"

Eleanor shook her head. "You've heard that, I know," she said. "But it isn't so. John worked with them—yes. Long before Sanchow he had lost his faith in the old China, and he thought perhaps the new one might be better. He was wrong, of course. And he found out that he was wrong. He's lost his faith in that, just as in everything else." Suddenly she put her hands to her face. "In himself. In other men. Even in faith itself—"

I went back to her.

"So you went on to Ningsia," I said.

She nodded.

"Why Ningsia?"

"Because—" She hesitated. "Because there had been an epidemic there. There was need for trained people. He thought we could be of help."

"But there was more to it than that?"

She didn't answer.

"What was it?" I demanded. "What was the real reason?"

"I—I don't know," she murmured.

"Yeng said that he seemed to be *waiting* for something."

She looked at me, almost sharply. For a moment her lips moved, but no words came out. Then—

"I don't know," she repeated.

And there was a pause.

"In Ningsia," I said gently "—what was he like? What did he do?"

"He saw the sick. He helped me with my work."

"And when he wasn't working?"

"He was alone a lot. You remember, perhaps, that the Great Wall lay just west of the town? He used to take a pony and ride out beyond it into the desert."

"Looking for something?"

"No. He said he simply wanted to see it. To feel it." Eleanor paused. "And at night, when he came home, he would sit, hour after hour, by the window —listening."

"Listening? To what?"

"To the wind," she said. "The wind blowing out of the desert."

"Then what finally happened?"

"Then finally one night he turned and said to me that we must go on again. . . . Go where? I asked. . . . On to the west, he said. Into the desert. Into its center, its heart."

"And so you left Ningsia."

"Two days later. He didn't tell anyone. He didn't go to the commissariat. There was a caravan going out, and we simply went with it."

"Leaving Yeng?"

"Yes, leaving Yeng. He was away in a neighboring village, and I said we must wait for him—we couldn't leave him. But John said, yes, we must. This was our journey; ours only; we must make it alone. And at last I saw it was a matter of either leaving Yeng or not going with John. So we left him a little money and moved on again. . . ."

Her voice trailed off. The lamplight flickered on

her face. I got up again and walked to the window and stood looking out into the darkness. . . . And, suddenly, I too was listening. . . . To the wind. The wind in the night. The wind humming softly through the streets of the old desert town.

Then I turned, and Eleanor was beside me.

"I haven't told you, Frank—" she murmured. "I *can't* tell you. Your being here: what it means to me—"

I bent and smiled a little and kissed her on the cheek.

"That you've come all this way for us," she said. "Only for us. Across the whole of China—"

"I was worried about you."

"And that you found us: it's a miracle." She paused, and when she spoke again her voice was barely audible. "Perhaps that's what he's been waiting for—all that can save him. A miracle—"

Her body was tense. For the first time she was losing control.

"You're tired, Elly," I said. "We're both tired." I put my hands on her shoulders. "We'll talk more tomorrow; talk it all out. And when he gets back—"

"Yes—when he gets back—"

Then it happened. The thing I had never seen before. A sudden sob wrenched her body, and her head bent forward against my chest. Leaning against me, she cried and cried and cried.

In the morning a dozen or so townspeople, mostly women and children, appeared, and Eleanor treated them in a makeshift dispensary. Yeng, almost unrecognizable in a white coat he had conjured from his saddle-bag, helped her quietly and deftly, as if his duties had never been interrupted.

Later, she sat in the living room with the boy, Khitai, hearing his multiplication tables and helping him with his English reading. "He should be studying Mongolian," she told me. "Or at least Chinese. Lord knows what use he'll ever have for English. But there's nothing to teach him with."

She had beside her a pile of pamphlets of the Calvert Correspondence System, and on a shelf were a row of children's books in faded jackets. Taking one at random, I opened it. On the flyleaf, in large careful script was written: *Jean Bickel, her book. Take at your perrel.*

I went out and walked for an hour through the squalid streets. There was no wind now, the sun burned down, and a haze of dust hung motionless over the town. As on the previous day, it was full of activity, of crowds and camel-trains, of the sights and sounds and stenches of a mid-Asian trading post. But again I saw no uniforms, no five-starred flags, no signs of the new imperium.

"Where do the Reds keep themselves?" I asked Eleanor when I returned.

"There are no civilian officials yet," she said, "and the garrison's out on the far side of the town. So far they've been too busy with bandit tribes to bother much with anything else."

"I'm not anxious to be picked up by them."

"They hardly ever come into town. Keep away from the garrison and there's nothing to worry about."

More patients had come to the dispensary, and for a while I watched her at her work. As long as she was busy and needed she was much like her old self, and I was glad for her. But when, in the afternoon, I walked with her to the markets, she was again silent and abstracted, and her eyes kept moving off down the streets that led in from the desert.

The marketing done, she and Yeng set out on a

round of sick calls. Khitai, too, was off somewhere, and I was alone in the house. It was on a side street, several blocks from the stir of the central square, and the only sound was that of my footsteps, as I paced slowly from room to room. When I stopped pacing there was no sound at all. A suspended, almost trancelike stillness filled the air and sifted into my mind. I sat in a chair by the window and looked out at the dust and sunlight and mud walls of the adjoining houses, and presently they seemed no longer real, but merely images, depthless and frozen. For two months and two thousand miles I had journeyed westward; river and desert had flowed by, half a continent had flowed by. But now they had stopped flowing. Nothing moved; the journey was over; I had reached its end. . . . But what did its end mean? What was I doing there? What *could* I do there?

I went into the kitchen and out again. To my room and out again. There was the sound of hoof-steps in the street, and I returned quickly to the window, but it was only two herdsmen riding their ponies toward the marketplace.

Going to the shelf, I glanced at what was left of the Bickels' books. Not many, it appeared, had been salvaged from the disaster at Sanchow. The Bible was still there, a few of John's volumes of oriental philosophy, the row that had once been Jean's. For no reason I can think of I took down Kipling's *Kim* and began to read it. Apparently Jean had been a confirmed annotator, for on the margin of Page Ten was a pencilled *Golly!* and, a few pages later, *This is doutful.* After a while I put the book away and went back to my room, and for a few minutes I stood looking at the picture of The Three Wise Men that hung above the cot. . . . "That is faith," John Bickel had said. "That is hope. A child is born. . . ."

Now a child was dead.

I lay down on the cot and tried to sleep.

Supper was much the same as on the night before. Eleanor and Yeng spoke briefly of their round of sick-calls. I scraped my memory for incidents of my trip and speculated on the new war in Korea, of which Eleanor had not heard. Khitai kept his eyes fastened on my wristwatch and proudly announced the time at approximately one-minute intervals. When the dishes had been done the other two disappeared, and Eleanor and I sat together in the living room. For a while we made conversation. Or tried to. "We'll talk it all out," I had said; but it was not that easy. What, after all, could I say that would hold any meaning, any help, for her? A few selected platitudes? A brotherly lecture?

The wind rose and hummed softly in the street outside.

"Look, Elly—" I said at last.

But she seemed not to hear me. And watching her, sitting straight and motionless in her chair, I knew it was not only the past that was haunting her, but the present, too. She was not only sorrowful. She was distracted.

"He'll be back tomorrow," I said.

She nodded without answering.

"Surely there's nothing to worry about. You say he's been out to these villages before."

"Yes."

"And they're not far. Not out where there might be real danger."

"No."

"Any number of things could be keeping him. More fever cases than he'd expected. Some village problem. A new tribe in from the desert—"

Again she didn't answer. It was obvious that what was troubling her was not simply that her husband was a few days late in his usual rounds. I went over and sat beside her.

"What is it, Elly?" I asked. "What's worrying you so? Try to tell me."

For still another moment she was silent, her eyes averted. Then she turned and looked straight at me. She said softly, "I'm frightened."

Over the years I had seen Eleanor Bickel in many difficult, even dangerous, situations, but I had never before heard her say anything like that. Sitting beside her in that little room, I felt a thin finger of cold run down my spine.

"You think something has happened to John?" I said.

She nodded slowly.

"What? What *could* have happened that you wouldn't have heard about?"

"I—I don't know."

She tried to go on, but couldn't. I tried to draw her

out, but couldn't. She seemed unable to look at me, unable to listen; and then, suddenly, she went off into the kitchen, and when I followed her I found her scrubbing the pots and pans that had already been cleaned.

"I'm sorry, Frank," she said quietly. "I don't know what's the matter with me. In the morning I'll be all right."

Soon after, she excused herself and went up to her room.

The next day passed. And the next.

There were the dispensary patients and Khitai's lessons. There were the marketing and the sick-calls. And that was all there was. The rest was a vacuum, a void, and, at the center of the void, Eleanor—waiting. Like time itself, she seemed suspended, transfixed; still able to accomplish the routine round of her duties, but powerless to control, or even express, the dark presentiments that filled her.

Each evening I suggested that the next day we ride out to the villages together, but both times, after seeming to think it over, she decided against it. . . . "No," she said, "he will come. John will come". . . . It wouldn't be long before I was to understand her reluctance; but, at the time, I didn't. I was confused, almost annoyed. And then on the third morning, while she was in the dispensary, I spoke, on sudden impulse, to Khitai.

"How far is it to these villages?" I asked him.

"Only a few li," he said.

"You know the way?"

"But of course I know."

"All right—we're going."

The boy's face lit up. "Good! I will go and tell Mother."

"No, don't tell her. Come on."

We hired ponies at one of the depots in the main square and rode out of the town toward the east.

"Is the garrison this way?" I asked Khitai.

"No," he said, "it is to the west."

"Are any of the villages near the garrison?"

"No, they are to the north and east."

That much was good, I thought. It was possible, of course—indeed, it then seemed to me probable—that Bickel had in some way run afoul of Red officialdom; but I didn't want to run afoul of them myself until all other possibilities had been investigated. We rode east to the first village, northwest to a second, west to a third, north to the fourth. That was all there were, Khitai said, within many days of traveling.

Only two of them were actually villages in a permanent sense; the others were clusters of yurts, the immemorial hide tents of Central Asia, pitched by nomad tribes that were summering near Borba. All were surrounded by sparse pastureland, in which camels, ponies and sheep were foraging. And all smelled alike, of dried dung and cooking butterfat. Mindful of typhus, I didn't go into any of the houses or yurts, but made my inquiries of people moving about outside. Or, more accurately, Khitai made the inquiries for me, for the language of these Mongol herdsmen had as little resemblance to Chinese as to English.

Yes, they told me at the first village—a white man had been there. Tall and with fiery hair. He had talked with the headman, visited the sick and given them magic tablets. But when we questioned them more closely it developed that this had been some three weeks before: obviously when Bickel had been on his previous round.

It was the same at the next village. And the next. In the third one the group we spoke to even remembered Bickel by name, but were definite that it had been almost a whole moon since he had been there.

It seemed all but hopeless to go on to the fourth village. But we did.

This was one of the yurt encampments—and the smallest of the lot—situated at the far northern margin of Borba's pastureland. Beyond its dark huddle of tents the last shreds of green vanished, and the waste rolled on, brown and empty, to the empty sky. Here the one we questioned was the tribal headman himself, an old Mongol with slitted eyes and a face of seamed leather, whom we found sitting before the central yurt. . . . Had a white man been there? Yes. . . . A tall white man with red hair? Yes. . . . How long ago? The old man thought for a moment. . . .

"It is now six days," he said.

I had Khitai repeat the question.

"He says yes—six days," said the boy.

"He's sure it's not more?"

"Yes, he is sure it is not more."

What had the white man done there? Treated the sick?

No, he had not treated the sick.

What had he done?

He had bought two ponies and food and a small tent. Then he had ridden off on the caravan trail to the north.

Alone?

Yes, alone.

That was all we learned. The old man did not know where he had gone; or why. North of Borba, he said, there was only wasteland, until one reached the Altai Mountains, and, beyond the Altai, waste again, all the way to Ulan Bator in Outer Mongolia. He could not understand how a man would set out on such a journey alone. Even the large caravans made careful preparations before setting out, and, in this particular year, few were making the attempt at all.

Because of bandits, did he mean?

He shook his head. "No, the bandit tribes are now to the south and west. Even they now avoid the north. It is a bad time now in the north."

"Bad? How?"

"Because the Black Sands," he said, "are blowing."

"The Black Sands—?"

The old man nodded. "Each year now, for many years, the winds in the desert have blown harder. Out of the wastes beyond the Altai; out of the darkness beyond the desert. And this is the year when at last the sands blow with them. . . . Listen, white man. Listen, small boy. . . . If you listen well, perhaps you can hear."

We stood silently. I listened. I strained my ears into the emptiness beyond the circle of tents, but I heard no sound, no faintest stirring in the stillness.

"Or perhaps you cannot," murmured the old man. "There are those, it is said, who cannot hear them until the sands are already sifting into their minds and hearts. . . ."

His thin voice trailed off. His eyes were almost closed. When we spoke again he did not seem to hear, and after a few moments we moved off. As we mounted our ponies, he was sitting as we had left him: his face to the north, motionless, listening.

"Mr. Knight—"

"Yes, Yeng?"

He had obviously been watching for me, for, as we neared the house, he had slipped from the door and come quickly along the street. "May I speak with you, sir?" he asked.

"Of course."

Khitai went on into the house. Yeng and I turned and walked down the block, and I could see that he was deeply agitated.

"What is it?" I asked him.

"It is about Mrs. Bickel." He hesitated. "You have noticed, of course, that she is most upset?"

I nodded. "About Mr. Bickel."

"Yes, about Mr. Bickel." There was another pause. "There is something I think you should know, Mr. Knight," he said. "She has received a message."

I stopped and stared at him. "A message? From him?"

"Yes."

"What did it say?"

"I do not know what it said. It was brought by a driver from an incoming caravan, and it was I who received it and gave it to her. But she did not show it to me or tell me what was in it."

"How do you know it was from Mr. Bickel?"

"Because I know his writing. And it was his on the outside."

"This happened today?"

"No, not today," said Yeng. "It is now three days ago."

"Three days! And she hasn't—"

"No, she has not told me anything. And I have had reason to believe, Mr. Knight, that she has not told you either."

I shook my head.

"That is why I have come to you," he said. "Until now I have waited. The message was for her alone— from her husband—and it seemed her right to do as she wished." Yeng paused again. "But now—now it seems no longer right. You have seen how she is. So distraught. So withdrawn. Since I have known her— even in Sanchow, when the little girl was killed—I have never seen her so. . . ."

As he spoke, my thoughts moved back, gropingly,

over those last few days. To Eleanor sitting at night in the little room, silent and haunted. To that one chilling moment when her eyes had met mine and she had whispered, "I'm frightened." To the shell that had again closed around her; her unwillingness—or inability—to speak her thoughts; her refusal to go out to the villages to make inquiries.

". . . . And so I have come to you," Yeng was saying. "Whatever it is that Mr. Bickel has written— where he has gone, what he is doing—these things she must tell us. To keep them to herself is no good. She will be sick. She will break down. Instead, she must tell us and we will help her."

His eyes were fixed anxiously on my face.

"Yes, Yeng," I said, "we must try to help her."

THIRTEEN

"Did you have a busy day?" Eleanor asked at supper.

"Yes, rather," I said.

"Exploring the town?"

"We hired two ponies and rode out a way."

"Oh. . . . Well, you had the best guide in Borba." She looked at Khitai, half severely, half smiling. "And the best hookey-player," she added.

"I am sorry, Mother," said the boy. "But you see, I thought it was Sunday, and—"

"Yes, of course—you thought it was Sunday. That makes tomorrow Monday, then, and we'll celebrate with double lessons."

"I'm afraid that I'm the guilty one," I put in.

"All right," said Eleanor, "we'll think up some lessons for you too."

For a few minutes, there at the table, she seemed relaxed and at ease. Once or twice she even smiled. The old smile. The wonderful smile. But soon the strain showed; the conversation flagged; and for the rest of the meal she sat without speaking, her eyes fixed vacantly on her plate. A while later, as on the previous nights, Yeng and Khitai left, and she and I were again alone in the living room. She adjusted the oil lamps, and I went to the window and stood looking out into the thickening dusk. Almost as I watched, it became night. Somewhere a camel brayed and another answered. Then they were quiet, and the only sound was the low hum of the wind.

When I turned, Eleanor was sitting on the sofa. I went and sat down beside her.

"We went out to the villages today," I said.

"The villages?"

"Yes. Khitai and I. We went looking for John."

She didn't say anything. She didn't look at me.

"In one of them," I said "—in the last nomad camp out to the north—we found someone who had seen him."

I waited.

"Are you listening, Elly?"

"Yes," she murmured, "I'm listening."

I told her what the old headman had said, and still she sat motionless and expressionless. Then I said:

"But you know this already—don't you?"

Now at last she moved. Her eyes met mine. Her body was rigid.

"Don't you, Elly?"

"How do you—"

"I've learned about the message," I said gently. "Yeng told me. He had to tell me."

"But I—"

"Yes, I know. You didn't want me to learn. You didn't want anyone." I put my hand on her arm. "But that's no good, Elly. Don't you see that? Whatever it is—however you feel—you can't go something like this alone."

She closed her eyes. For a long moment she didn't answer. Then she said: "I've wanted to tell you, Frank. Truly I have. Every day since it came—every night that we've sat here—I've told myself, yes, I must tell you, I must speak to you. Only—"

"Only what?"

"Only it seemed too incredible. Too awful. You've come all these miles to be with us; to help us. And now—"

Her voice was no more than a whisper. Then it faded altogether. She tried to turn away, but my hand tightened on her arm.

"What was the message?" I said quietly. "What did he say?"

For several seconds she sat perfectly still, and I could see that she was making a tremendous effort to control herself. Then she rose, crossed to a small desk that stood in the corner and took out a slip of paper. Returning, she handed it to me.

I held it in the flickering light of the oil lamp. The paper was creased and yellowed, but the pencilled writing was unmistakably in Bickel's hand. *Forgive me, my dearest*, it read, *but this is a thing I must do. Whatever the journey, whatever the cost, I must find what is beyond the Black Sands. God bless and keep you. John.*

Now it was my turn to sit voiceless and motionless. Eleanor stood looking down at me.

"What does it mean?" I said at last.

"I'm not sure," she murmured.

I had not raised my head. I stared at the pencilled words as if suddenly they might rearrange themselves into clarity and meaning.

"The Black Sands—"

"Have you heard of them?" said Eleanor.

"Only today. From the old headman." With an effort I looked up. "I assumed they were some sort of Mongol legend."

Eleanor nodded. "Yes, they are part of an old legend. One can't be long in this part of the world without hearing about them."

"What are they? What's John talking about?"

She sat down. She was calmer now, or at least more controlled, and I knew that, if nothing else, speaking out would help her state of mind. For a long moment she was silent, as if deep in thought, and when she spoke again it was to ask a question.

"Do you know the name Karakorum?" she said.

I repeated the word. "Wasn't it the old capital of the Mongol Empire?" I asked.

She nodded. "Karakorum was the capital of Genghis Khan. It was the city from which he and his armies set out to conquer the world. After his death it was destroyed, and never rebuilt, but its ruins still stand in the desert about three hundred miles north of Borba. In the Mongolian language Karakorum means Black Sands."

I let this sink in. Then I asked, "But how does it concern John? He's not an archaeologist or historian."

Eleanor didn't answer.

"Beyond the Black Sands—" I mused.

I looked at her, waiting.

"Why?" I demanded. "Why did he go? Why do you *think* he went?"

When she spoke again it was with a quietness that was in almost frightening contrast to the turmoil of emotions that I knew was within her. "I'm almost afraid to say this, Frank," she said, "and I'm saying it only because you're an old friend and know that I'm not an hysterical person. I don't think John wanted to go at all. At least not in the way we usually think of wanting." She paused. "I believe that he had to go. That something was *pulling* him there."

I started to speak, but she stopped me. "Let me finish," she said. "Then if you think I'm insane you can say so. I don't know how much chance you've had to notice it yet, but the Mongols are deeply imaginative people. As far as formal religion goes, most of them are Buddhists, but their Buddhism is mixed up with all sorts of beliefs and legends that are older than any religion in the world. Mostly, as with all primitive people, their superstitions have to do with the unknown; with the fear of darkness and death." She paused again and looked at me with a curious expression. "This old headman you met today—what did he tell you about the Black Sands?"

"He said they were blowing. That this was the year for their blowing, or something of the sort, and that the caravans avoided them."

"He didn't speak of Karakorum?"

"No."

"Or say what the sands are supposed to be?"

"No."

"John and I had heard of them years ago," she said. "When we first came to China and he began studying its history. And now we've heard of them again from some of the people out here. The way they tell it, the sands form a great wasteland around the ruins of the old city. They say that the land is the most barren in the world—worse even than the Gobi Desert, to the east. In the time of Genghis Khan the land was fertile black earth, but over the centuries the rivers have dried up, the rocks and trees have crumbled, the same as the city itself, and no living thing, plant, animal or man, can exist there. That, they say, is why Karakorum has never been rebuilt and why the caravans and nomad tribes avoid it. The legend is that the sands were formed by the decomposed bodies of the millions of men killed by

Genghis and his armies. They call them the Sands of Death."

Eleanor sat silently for a moment, looking at me. "I know," she said, "that what I'm saying must sound strange, even demented, to you. You mustn't take it to mean that I believe in these superstitions. Or—" She hesitated. "Or John either."

"Did he ever talk about them?"

"In the old days, yes. You remember how interested he always was in the old Eastern myths and legends. I think he knew some of them as well as he did our own Bible stories, and sometimes, after reading them, he'd speculate on their origins and meanings."

"Has he been doing that recently?"

"No, recently not at all. As I told you, Frank, he's changed—so terribly. During the past few months it was almost impossible to get him to talk about anything. Anything inside him, that is. In the daytime it wasn't too bad. He helped me with my work; he kept busy. But when night came we'd sit in this room together, hour after hour, and he wouldn't say a word. He wouldn't even read, as he always used to. He no longer asked me to play the organ. He'd just sit, that was all; sit in that chair over there by the window, hour after hour; looking out . . . and listening."

Again I felt the thin finger, the furtive coolness on my spine. And for an instant it was not Eleanor's face I saw before me, but another face, yellow and old; the face and figure of the Mongol headman, hunched before his yurt, staring out at the wasteland with sunken eyes.

"There were times," said Eleanor, "when I felt I couldn't bear it any longer. I'd go over to him and kneel beside him and say, 'Talk to me, John. Please talk to me.' And he'd take my hand, but say nothing. 'Hold me in your arms,' I'd say; and he'd hold me. But he wasn't there. Whatever it was he was thinking and suffering, he couldn't share it—even with me."

"And he said nothing before he left?"

"Only the usual things. The same as whenever he went off to the villages."

"Yet you knew that this time it was different?"

"I—I'm not sure." She hesitated. "No, that's not true. I *did* know. Not in my mind, maybe—but somehow—"

"And when the message came, you knew what it was going to say?"

She didn't answer. I stood up and put my hands gently on her shoulders.

"How, Elly?" I asked. "How did you know? What made you so sure he had gone to Karakorum?"

Her eyes looked back at me: distraught, almost feverish. Suddenly she tried to turn away.

"Tell me, Elly. You must tell me."

She stood still. She struggled for control. Then she said quietly: "I think he went because he had to go. Because he was convinced that something was *happening* out there."

"Happening?" The word jerked out of my mouth. "What do you mean—happening?"

She put a hand to her eyes. "I don't know," she murmured. "I don't know. It's all fantastic, of course. And yet—" She faltered and stopped.

"Go on," I said.

"Yet I believe what I said before. That something is—pulling him."

"But in God's name, what? Haven't you any idea?"

Her hand still covered her eyes, and her head was bent. "Yes, I have an idea," she said softly. "I think he has heard the sound of the Black Sands blowing."

I felt my hands tighten against her shoulders. I heard the hum of the wind in the street outside. And now, suddenly, Eleanor Bickel raised her head and looked straight at me, and any suspicion of her mental state which may have nudged my mind was gone, instantly and for good. There was the same blue, steady sanity in her eyes that had always been there. Except that added to it now was a cold, consuming fear. . . .

"I think he has heard it," she said, "because I have heard it myself."

Later, in the darkness, I sat alone on the steps of the house. The street was silent and deserted, and above the mud roofs of the town the constellations burned in the black brilliance of the night. Between them and the earth a thin tide of air flowed smooth and unvarying from the north. My mind fumbled among the strange bypaths into which it had been led in the hours just past. . . . The sound of the Black Sands blowing? . . . Almost in spite of myself, I strained my senses into the murmur of the nightwind. Its sound, I thought, was the same as that of any other wind: a faint crackling in the leaves of the dry trees, a whisper of sliding flowing air against the walls of the house. But even as I thought it, I was no longer sure. Perhaps it was a quality that was in the wind itself, or perhaps it was merely in the tired straining of my mind; but somewhere in that vast dome of night something I did not know or wish to know had its existence and communicated itself to me. Softly, sadly, like a whisper carried down the dark streets from the desert beyond, there came to me the sound of the ancient darkness of the heart of Asia.

My room was black and airless. The window opened on a courtyard where the wind did not penetrate, but the nameless stenches of the old city seemed to creep through it and fill the room like tangible presences. The minutes crawled by, and then the hours, as I turned and twisted and fought for sleep. But there was no sleep. The harder I struggled to compose body and mind, the more restlessly and feverishly the blood pounded through my flesh. It almost seemed that as if by some unholy chemistry the fantastic thoughts of that night had transferred themselves into physical impulses and were crowding one another through every nerve and artery of my body. Over and over, the words of Eleanor Bickel repeated themselves in my mind, until they were as distorted and grotesque as the sounds and images of a nightmare. Presently it seemed as if every inch of me was on fire: not only flesh, but blood and bones as well. And then again I heard the wind. It was not in the room nor in the courtyard outside, but in my ears, my head, my body. Starting as a deep, soft humming, it grew slowly into a monstrous tide of sound and darkness. . . .

FOURTEEN

That night may have held the first forewarning of typhus. I don't know. What I do know is that it marked the beginning of experiences which I now half believe did not happen at all, but were in some way merely a strange fabrication of fever.

The next morning, however, I was apparently all right. It was Eleanor who appeared pale and strengthless—almost ill—and it was obvious that she had passed a sleepless night. She went through her usual round of duties: in the dispensary, with Khitai at his lessons, cleaning and ordering the house. But her responses were mechanical, her mind was elsewhere; and I knew that her talking with me, far from exorcising her fears, had heightened them to a point where they were almost unendurable. Several times I tried to speak with her, to reassure her, to get her at least to lie down and rest. But she merely shook her head or murmured something about "work to be done," and went on with what she was doing.

I told Yeng what little I had learned the night before, and toward noon we went together to the central square. There, in the trading depots, we inquired as to what caravans had arrived, during the past few days, from the north. There had been only one, we were told: that of a Turki hide-merchant bound from Mongolia to Western Tibet. And it had moved on south from Borba three days before, after a stop-over of only one night. The camel driver who had brought Bickel's message was gone and vanished. As if he had never been.

When I returned to the house Eleanor and Khitai were out. Taking the message from the drawer where Eleanor had replaced it, I examined it again. . . . *Whatever the journey, whatever the cost, I must find what is beyond the Black Sands.* . . . The writing was not merely recognizable as Bickel's; it was exactly as I remembered it. Firm, clear, a shade schoolmasterish, with no sign of haste or strain. It might as well have read, *Meet me at the Y handball court at five.*

I put the note away.

That's it, I told myself: think of the handball. Think of how he laughed, how he cracked his knuckles, how he liked spare ribs and Chinese noodles. Whatever's happened to him—whatever he's been through—he's still John Bickel. Not a spectre, not a phantom, not a ghost. He's still John Bickel, six-foot-three, 220-pounds, of Nebraska, U.S.A., and if he's gone off to something called the Black Sands, near some place called Karakorum, in the heart of nowhere, he's had a damn good reason for doing it.

I looked at the window, and the sun was shining. I looked around the room, and it was neat, familiar, almost cheerful. All right, I thought: he came to Borba. Now he has gone to Karakorum. . . .

Going to my room, I got my map, unfolded and bent over it. There was Borba, tiny and lost, at almost the very center of Asia. There to the north were the Altai Mountains, and, beyond them, northeast, the towns of inhabited Mongolia. But between these there was nothing. Even the dotted line that marked the old caravan route, veered suddenly away, once it had crossed the Altai, leaving only an expanse of blank brown emptiness.

Back in the living room, I rummaged along the shelves. Presumably Bickel had taken some sort of map with him, but there might also be something left; and presently I found it. It was an old mold-eaten atlas, printed in English, more than fifty years ago, in Shanghai, and on its map of Western China was what I was looking for. Again there was Borba, the Altai, Mongolia, the caravan route; but here, in the blank space beyond, was also a cluster of dots and, in minute letters, the words *Ruins of Karakorum*. Using the scale, I measured the distance down to Borba, and, as Eleanor had said, it was almost three hundred miles. Roughly a four-hour round trip by plane, I thought. But as many weeks by camel or pony. Even if he did nothing but go and return, Bickel could not possibly be back in less than a month. Assuming that that was where he had gone.

I put the atlas back.

Assuming. . . .

What else could one assume? What else could the note have meant? . . . *I must find what is beyond the Black Sands.* . . . For a long time I sat alone: thinking, musing. When at last I looked up, the sun had set and a low wind had risen in the street outside.

"Frank—"

"Yes?"

"I was in the marketplace this afternoon," she said. "There's a caravan leaving tomorrow for Ningsia."

"Ningsia?"

She hesitated. Then—"I—I think you should go with it," she said.

Her voice was quiet. Her face, in the lamplight, was still tired and drawn, but the tenseness was gone from her body, the haunting fear from her eyes. She was calmer and more controlled than I had seen her at any time since my arrival.

"No, Elly," I told her. "I'm staying a while."

She came over and sat beside me. "Your coming here, Frank—" she said "—all this way, across China—

to find us: I can't tell you what it's meant to me. What it will mean to John. . . . But—you can't stay here—don't you see? You have your own life; your work; you have to go back to them. And it may be weeks before John—"

I was shaking my head and she stopped. "Please, Frank," she said. "It's the only thing. You must—"

"I'm staying here with you," I told her.

"But—" She paused and looked away, and I could see that she was struggling with something within herself. . . . Then she said it:

"But—you see—I'm not staying—"

"Not staying?"

"I'm going after him. To look for him."

"No, Elly—you can't! It's hundreds of miles—across the desert—"

"I've been in the desert before," she said. "I'll take Yeng or Khitai; perhaps a couple of other men; and ponies—"

"And even if you get there, he may be already gone. You may miss him entirely."

There was a pause; Eleanor shook her head slowly. "No, Frank—no," she said. "Ever since the message came—even before that: ever since I first suspected where he was going—I've been asking myself, what shall I do?—what shall I do? Now at last I know. It's to go after him. I *have* to go after him."

"But it—it's—" I reached for the word and didn't find it. "You must stay here, Elly," I told her. "Wait for him. Be patient. In a few weeks he'll be back."

"No," she said again, and for a moment her voice

had the same strange timbre that it had held the previous night. "That's the point. The whole point. I'm not at all sure he'll be back."

I argued; I reasoned; I tried in every way I could think of to pry her from her fears and premonitions into what was "sensible" and "practical" and "objective." But even as I spoke I knew that there was no chance of dissuading her. Her mind was made up. More than her mind, her heart and soul were made up. I could no more have stopped her than I could. . . . (I remember pausing, listening). . . . than I could have stopped the wind from blowing in the night beyond the windows.

At last I gave up. For a few minutes we sat in silence. And when I spoke again it was, as so often in the two months past, without consciousness of having thought it out or reached a decision. I simply said:

"Then I'll go with you."

Now of course it was her turn to protest; but this time it was I who was unmovable. I was not going with the caravan, in any case. Indeed, it was my plan, when I did move on, not to return at all to eastern China (where I was sure to be arrested and deported), but to go south and west until I came out in India or Pakistan. Such a trip would take months, and what did a few more weeks matter? Particularly if those weeks were for the sake of the two people I cared most for in the world. "Do you think I've come two thousand miles to find you and John, "I asked her, "only to walk out on you now?"

"But—"

"But nothing," I said.

And in the end she accepted my decision, as I had accepted hers. She stood up and walked across the room and then came back and again sat beside me. She rested her head on my shoulder, and I held her hand. And though she didn't speak, her hand spoke; all her loneliness, her fear, her gratitude were in its gentle pressure; and for a long time we sat there silently in the lamplit room.

In the two years that have passed I have often thought back to that night; to the two of us there together; to the decisions that we made. I search my mind and heart for what else I could have said and done. And I find nothing. "I have to go," she had said. And if she had to, so did I. Even with the after-knowledge of the strange and terrible things that were to come, I don't see how I could have done otherwise.

Our arrangements were quickly made. In two days we had assembled the necessary food, tents and equipment and bought eight sturdy Mongolian ponies. We found a half-dozen large goatskin bags for our all-important water supply, and over Eleanor's protests—for she hated firearms—I picked up two ancient Mauser rifles and some ammunition. After some discussion it was decided that Yeng would stay in Borba: partly because a one-armed man would obviously have a hard time on such a journey, partly because someone was needed to take care of the house and run the dispensary. But Khitai—to his vociferous joy—was to come along as general helper, and from the caravan depot we hired two strong young Mongols as packers and porters.

From the moment we set to work Eleanor was a different woman: busy, efficient, sometimes almost cheerful, absorbed in the details of selecting, checking and packing. Once—only once—when the day's work was done and we were alone in the evening, did she again question my coming and said, "Frank, are you sure—?"

"Yes, I'm sure," I said.

And that was the end of it.

We filled the saddle-bags. We filled the water-bags. And at the end of the second day, with everything done, we sat together in the living room and for the first time played a game of hearts, as we had sometimes done years before in Peiping and Shanghai.

"If we're lucky," I told her, "do you know what's going to happen? After a few days on the trail we're going to meet John on his way back."

"I hope so," she murmured. "Oh, I hope so."

Not once, during those last two days, did I catch the dark haunted look in her eyes. Not once did she speak of old Mongol legends, or Black Sands, or of her having "heard" them in the night.

In the half-light of an early morning we started off. Yeng stood disconsolately in the doorway and waved his one arm. Then we moved on down the street and he was gone. Khitai had leapt into his saddle and trotted ahead, like a commander leading his troops.

Then came Eleanor and I and, in the rear, the two porters with the pack ponies. We rode through the central square and out along the main caravan trail to the north, and, as the sun rose, the dun walls of Borba dwindled behind us into the flatness of the land. When I glanced at Eleanor her head was bent, and I guessed that she was praying. But after a moment she looked up and smiled a little, and we rode on side by side.

During that first morning we were on the route that Khitai and I had followed a few days before, and after an hour we passed through one of the two permanent outlying villages. Then there was a wide belt of stunted shrubs and sword grass and a chain of brown waterless lake-beds, ringed with miles of reeds. Beyond these, in turn, were sparse grazing land and the nomad camp where I had talked to the old headman; and, passing the central yurt, I saw him sitting motionless before it, exactly as he had been before. Then the camp, too, was gone, and ahead there was nothing. Nothing but the long trail of the caravan track creasing the brown floor of the desert.

Toward midday we stopped for two hours and rested; then moved on until it was almost dark. We pitched the tents, cooked supper, ate, slept, and at dawn we moved on again. Day followed day, without variation. It was now late August; the early fall would soon be coming to the high plateaus, and when night came it grew suddenly cold. During the day, however, the sun hung hot and malignant in the parched sky. And, day and night, the thin wind blew from the north, driving the sand into our faces and the crevices of our clothes.

Twice during the first week we met caravans moving southward, and both times we stopped them and made inquiries. But nothing came of them. At long intervals, the travelers reported, they had passed caravans moving north, but they had seen no white man with them, and no man at all traveling alone. We thanked them and moved on. The sun rose and set over the empty land.

Some details of that journey have already faded from my memory. Others remain. Clearest of all is the memory of Eleanor Bickel.

By that time I had known her, on and off, for twelve years, but in retrospect I feel as if I had never *really* known her until now. There is only one word to describe her, and that is "heroic." I knew that she had no genuine hope of meeting John on his return journey; sometimes I felt that she had no hope of finding him at all. But she was calm, patient, thinking always of the rest of us rather than of herself. In camp, she insisted on preparing all the meals. She treated us for cuts, bruises and windburn. And not once, however hard the day or dismal the night, did she speak a word of complaint. If not with her husband, she was now at least following him—searching for him. And if that did not bring her happiness, it at least gave her a reason for being.

Khitai remained in high spirits: a slant-eyed, button-nosed imp. Ordinarily I can either take twelve-year-olds or leave them, but he was a fine antidote to the stillness and monotony of the trip. The two porters, on the other hand, were silent and sullen. We had had no trouble with them yet, and they did their work; but they were obviously not happy at having come.

Sun—sky—space. The days followed each other, as identical as the beads on a blue necklace. Toward noon one day there was a quick savage sandstorm; then, again, sun and stillness. That afternoon, at last, the brown flatness ahead began to undulate, and faint peaks and notches showed on the distant horizon. . . . The Altai? . . . Yes, said the porters, they were the Altai. And through the next day they drew nearer. We were now obviously out of China and in the Outer Mongolian Republic, but governments and frontiers had no more meaning here than on the bottom of an ocean. Since the second caravan we had seen no signs of life. Man and his works were as remote as if they were on another planet, lost and forgotten beyond the gulfs of space.

Presently we entered the foothills of the Altai. The peaks were bare, eroded, unimaginably old, looking less like mountains than the stumps of prehistoric pyramids. The porters said that in winter, when snow fell, streams flowed down from them; but now they were as dry and desolate as the surrounding desert.

For a day we were pinned down in our tents, while the wind blew a gale. Eleanor and I dozed, played hearts, sat and waited, with occasional sorties outside to dig at the sanddrifts that threatened to bury us. Toward evening the wind dropped, then vanished altogether, and after the hours of frenzied howling the night seemed filled with an almost monstrous stillness. The stars were bigger and brighter than I had ever seen them. One particularly—Polaris? —The Pole Star?—burned like a white flare in the northern sky.

We plodded on again. First through stillness; then through wind. We crossed a low pass through the Altai and descended the far slope. On either side the mountains rose, scarred and forlorn, and ahead the waste stretched again, limitless, to the horizon. Staring at the desolation, I found myself suddenly, ludicrously, trying to whistle. But the wind rammed the feeble effort back into my teeth.

We wound on through the northern foothills. Slowly. Doggedly. Eleanor was still the same—which was wonderful; Khitai quieter, but all right. As for the porters, I wasn't sure. Each morning I expected trouble, but it didn't materialize. And through the day they rode, hunched and silent, into the wind.

It was now September: the month the Mongols call *The Season of Endings.*

Well, we would see.

Late on the tenth day, beyond the Altai, we reached the point where the trade route bent sharply east toward Ulan Bator and Central Mongolia. And there, camped for the night in the dry bed of a stream, was the third southbound caravan we had met since leaving Borba.

Pitching our own tents nearby, we went over and asked the usual questions. And at first received the usual answers. They had left Ulan Bator two weeks before and in that time had passed three caravans going in the opposite direction. . . . All toward the east? Yes, all toward the east. . . . Except one, someone presently recalled—a fourth one they had almost forgotten—too small to be called a caravan, really, but merely a string of a few men and animals, scarcely bigger than our own.

And which way had *it* been going?

"North," said the caravan leader. "It was not following a trail at all, but came up out of the desert to the south, camped near us for a night and went on into the desert the next morning."

"How long ago was that?"

"About four days."

"And where was it going?"

The trader shrugged. "That is what we could not understand, for to the north there is nothing. Only the wastes." He paused. "Only the Black Sands. . . ."

"They didn't explain?"

"No, they did not explain. They were not a usual caravan, you see. They were lamas—from Tibet— and they said merely that they were on a pilgrimage to the north. One does not ask too many questions of holy lamas. We gave them food and water, and then they blessed us and moved on."

Back at our tents we cooked our supper and sat close around the fire in the darkness. We slept. And in the morning we too moved on. Not eastward along the caravan trail—but north; no longer on one of the great trade routes of Central Asia, but across a trackless wasteland into which few men had ventured for centuries past. The other caravan vanished behind us. The peaks of the Altai vanished behind us. I guided our course with a tin compass that I had bought in the bazaar at Borba.

All day we crept northward under the sun. . . .

FIFTEEN

. . . . and when the sun set we camped again. Night fell. The stars blazed. Between stars and earth the wind blew, thin and cold, from the north. In the darkness of my tent I could hear it humming across the empty miles. And in the morning, what I had been expecting happened.

When I stepped from the tent I found the two porters squatting on the ground outside. They arose as I appeared and stood facing me, obviously ill at ease. Finally it was Aktar, the older of the two, who spoke.

"You will go on north, sir?" he asked.

"Yes," I said.

Aktar looked at the ground. "We will not go," he said softly.

"Won't go?" I repeated. "What do you mean? Why?"

"The Black Sands are blowing."

There was a pause.

"I have seen no black sand," I said.

The man stooped, picked up a handful of sand and held it toward me. It was mostly brown, the same dun-brown of the wasteland through which we had crept for so many days; but mixed in with it were a few minute black particles.

I took a pinch of grains between my fingers and examined it closely. "All right," I said, "there is some black sand. What of it?"

"They are the Sands of Death," said Aktar.

Through the long hours of the morning I wrangled and cajoled, bribed and threatened. The two Mongols were obdurate. They would go with us, they said, to the ends of the earth, if we would return to the caravan route and bear east, or even west across the trackless barrens; but they would not move so much as another inch to the north. Eleanor pleaded with them. Even Khitai tried his hand, in a quick guttural dialect I could not understand. But still with no result. I believe I could have brought out one of the Mausers and shot them down where they stood, before they would have moved. By midafternoon we had to face the fact that it was hopeless. I told them they could take two of the mules and enough food to carry them back to Borba. Then, as the sun sloped toward the brown horizon, we stood silently in front of the tents and watched them plod out of sight toward the south.

It was too late to go on that day. Sitting in front of the tents, Eleanor and I watched the harsh daylight fade and the bare table of the land pass slowly into the softer shades of evening. There was, I believe, no thought in either of our minds that we ourselves might turn back. Or if there was, we didn't express it. By this time we had come so far in our journey, both physically and in our imaginings, that such considerations as our whereabouts, food supply and personal safety seemed almost irrelevant. We were caught and held captive by the spell of our fantastic improbable search.

It was that evening, I think, that marked the beginning of the strange lassitude—the sense of suspension, of unreality—that was to remain with me almost constantly during the days to come. The porters were gone: all right. We would go on alone: all right. It didn't matter. Sitting there in the dusk, I could feel a slackness, a languor, in my body and mind. My eyes wanted to close, my hands to fall open, palms upward, on my lap. It seemed almost as if the void of the desert were enveloping me, penetrating me, making me one with it. Beside me, Eleanor seemed to have fallen asleep, and for the first time it was Khitai, and not she, who began the preparations for supper. After a while I roused myself to help him, but Eleanor did not stir until I brought her her plate and cup.

"I—I'm sorry," she murmured, as if awakening.

"Easy does it," I told her.

We ate in silence. When we had finished it was dark and the stars were out. Before us the dung fire glowed—another star—tiny but alive in the black miles of the night.

It was perhaps four the next morning when I awoke and sat suddenly upright. I knew at once that it was a sound that had awakened me, but at first I had no intimation of what sort of sound. I sat still and listened. Outside the tent I could hear the soft shifting of the ponies and the creaking of their tethers. And beyond them was the low, changelessly familiar humming of the wind. That was all. Then, abruptly, I knew what it was that I had heard. It *was* the wind. The wind—or rather something that was in or behind the wind. As I listened now, the sound swelled until it filled my ears and throbbed in the channels of my brain. It was not loud, but low, persistent, pervading, and although its presence filled the tent, it seemed to be coming to me from very far away. It was the sound of moving air—there was no doubt about that—but of something else too: of the slow distant slur of shifting sand, perhaps; the beating of a deep rhythm upon the sand; the moving of a vast dark tide across the sand. It rose, undulated, fell; swept up out of the wind and subsided into it, behind it. Then it was gone. When at last I jerked aside the tent-flap and looked out into the night there was only the sky and the stars and the dark earth stretching quietly into distance.

At the first graying of the morning Khitai and I

struck the tents and began loading the ponies. Meanwhile Eleanor prepared breakfast, and by full daylight we were ready to go. Just as we were starting, however, Khitai gave a sharp cry, scrabbled quickly in the sand and came up with a small glinting object.

"It is your watch, sir!" he announced excitedly. "You have dropped your watch!"

I thanked him and took it from him, and then had a better idea. "No, you wear it, Khitai," I told him.

"*I*, sir?" He all but jumped in his excitement.

"Yes." With my knife I punched another hole in the strap and fastened it to his wrist. "You'll take better care of it than I."

"I will take the most greatest care," he promised. "And I will help too—you will see. With the compass you will make the direction, and with the watch now I will make the time."

Then we were on our way, and throughout the day he announced the half-hours as unfailingly as a ship's bell. For a while it gave me a rather pleasantly insane feeling. In that timeless waste, I thought, he might almost as well have been counting off the days or the weeks.

We crept on across the emptiness: through an endless parched monotony of sand and sky. Each hour was the same as the next, each mile the same as the next; time and movement seemed merely illusions. Yet I knew that by now we had come most of the way on our journey and that the ruins of Karakorum lay no more than fifty miles to the north. I spoke the name in my mind. . . . Karakorum. . . . And I think it was the first time I had done so in all our traveling. Whatever my thoughts, whatever the intimations and imaginings that flickered like shadows within me, I had kept them deep and controlled on the outer margins of consciousness. And so, too, had Eleanor—at least as far as I could tell—for not once had she spoken again of the dead city or the Black Sands or of the strange things she had told me that night in Borba. When we talked, it was of the day's march, the condition of the ponies, the next camp, the next meal, the next mile. And in the hours between we rode in silence.

Karakorum—I thought. But it was only a word; without meaning or reality. We rode in silence, and the only sound was the slurring of sand under the plodding hooves of the ponies.

Half the time I kept my eyes to the north, the other half to the east, searching for signs of the other caravan of which we had been told. If the information had been correct, its course lay in that direction. And if it, too, was bound for Karakorum (and where else *could* it be bound in that trackless waste?) its route and ours must eventually converge. But there was no sign of it. The rim of the land cut sharp and bare against the sky. And as the day wore on I stopped searching; the lethargy of the previous evening returned; I rode with eyes half-closed, and all there was between earth and sky was the rhythmic swaying of my pony and the wind blowing low and steady from the north.

"One o'clock," called Khitai.

"Half past one."

"Two."

His voice seemed faint and remote, like a voice heard in a dream. . . .

Toward midafternoon I struggled back to something resembling consciousness. The first thing I was aware of was that the wind had dropped, and then, looking about me, I saw that the earth itself was undergoing a gradual and subtle change. It was no longer a perfectly flat unbroken plane, but rose and fell in gentle waves; and its surface was swollen by low irregular mounds and scarred with fissures and the bare beds of long-dried streams. Also there were now rocks among the sand: huge naked shapes rising out of the earth like twisted gargoyles. Even the sand itself was different—heavier in texture and glittering darkly in the sun. Dismounting to scoop a few grains into my hand, I saw that it was almost black, like particles of hard coal.

Never had I seen or imagined so desolate a country. Far from mitigating the loneliness and lifelessness of the earth, the rocks and humps and the tortured undulation of the sand served rather to intensify it. It was such a prospect, I felt, as might confront a traveler among the craters of the moon. The emptiness of the true desert had been blank, open, with nothing to conceal; the emptiness here was of a different kind—ambiguous, suggestive, full of shapes and shadows and the secrets of years. The earth was now not merely a thing that had never been alive.

It was a corpse, transfixed and rotting in the sun. Any eventuality, any frightfulness or abomination, seemed possible here. A living thing—a man, a horse, a camel, even a buzzard or a creeping insect—was an anachronism, an intruder.

My eyes moved over the miles ahead. And my mind followed. I tried to picture those who had gone before us. . . . The lamas' caravan. . . . Bickel. . . . I saw John Bickel on a pony: his long legs almost touching the ground, his great shoulders hunched, the flaming thatch of his hair the only thing that shone, that lived, in all that world of lifeless emptiness. I saw him moving on, farther and farther, between the dunes and hummocks, across the black sand, toward . . . what? Suddenly I was thinking of Eleanor's words on that night in Borba. "He was convinced," she had said, "that something was happening out there."

Happening. . . .

Whatever it is that is happening, I thought, it must be a thing that *requires* this emptiness.

"Three," said Khitai.

"Half past three."

"Four."

We had passed through a hollow, skirted a mound. And now suddenly I stopped and stared incredulously ahead. It's a mirage, I thought. But it wasn't a mirage. It was a miracle.

It was a tree.

A single tree. No more than six feet high; without bark or leaves; stunted, warped, withered. Its roots were gripped around a black slab of rock. Its branches hung gnarled and frozen against the sky. It had been dead for years, perhaps for centuries; but still it was a tree. Once it had drawn life from the desert sun. Once it had sucked life from beneath the desert floor. We stopped and stared at it, and there it was.

"The Tree of Heaven," I said, and tried to smile.

We camped there. Two hours of daylight were left, but we camped anyhow. We unloaded the ponies and pitched the tents and again sat in front of them, watching the light fade slowly into the grayness of evening. In other deserts I had known the sun often set brilliantly, in a wild spectrum of color. But not here. Here there was only a fading, a thickening, a cold lengthening of shadow, a tree black and twisted against the dusk. I listened for the wind, but there was no wind. There was only stillness, immense and unbroken, and within the stillness within myself—the deep listlessness, the torpor, that I had experienced before. Perhaps this was a forewarning of germinating fever; again I don't know. All I remember is the lethargy, the emptiness; the black sands seeming to envelop me, as they enveloped the earth around us.

I looked at Eleanor. Throughout the day's march she had been the same as always: patient, enduring, uncomplaining. But now, as on the previous evening, all strength seemed to have drained from her. Her face was sallow and slack; there were dark streaks of sand in the hollows beneath her eyes, the eyes themselves seemed lustreless, burnt out. We sat in silence.

I picked up a handful of sand and let it run slowly between my fingers.

Then, abruptly, I stood up.

"Tonight, mem sahib—" I tried the smile again "—we dress for dinner."

In the tent I actually did change shirt and trousers, and then, by the light of a tallow lamp, I shaved my week-old beard. It was hard going. The skin underneath was chafed and raw; the razor seemed to catch at every stroke, and when I put my hand to my face it came away stained with blood. But on that night, in that place, this didn't annoy me. On the contrary, I remember holding my hand up before me and looking at it with a strange satisfaction. The blood was warm, it was red and thick, it was the stuff of life. In the gray stillness of that world beyond the world, I was almost grateful that I was still human enough, alive enough, to bleed.

When I came out it was full night. A small fire was going, and Eleanor and Khitai were preparing supper. She too, I saw, had freshened herself and partially changed her clothes, and seemed to have regained some of her strength. But she was still withdrawn and abstracted, and we ate in almost complete silence.

"Half past seven," said Khitai.

And a while later, "Eight."

Then he went into his tent, and Eleanor and I sat alone. For a while we talked desultorily: about the day's march, the next day's, our water supply, the sores on the ponies' legs. Or, rather, I talked and Eleanor listened, occasionally answering, more often merely nodding when I paused. Since we had finished supper she had scarcely moved. Her head was tilted back a little, and I knew she was staring at the warped tree and the night beyond.

"Talk, Elly," I said. "Whatever you're thinking, tell me. It will help."

"I was thinking," she said softly, "of a night, many years ago, when John and I sat together under a tree. It wasn't a tree like this at all. It was a dogwood tree, in blossom, on a June night in Sedalia, Missouri. John had graduated that day from divinity school, and been ordained; and I'd come there to be with him, and the next day we were going to be married. It was the most beautiful night I had ever known. I was happier than I had ever been. Everyone else had gone to bed, and for a long time we sat there, just John and I, under this tree near the edge of the campus. I remember, my head was on his shoulder, we were holding hands, and we didn't talk—there was no need to talk—and I just sat there beside him, in my happiness, until—until suddenly I realized that something had changed. Perhaps it was something in his face—I don't know. Or in the touch of his hand. But all at once I had the feeling that he was—well—no longer *there*. And I remember the quick little coldness inside me, and I waited a while, and then I looked up at him and asked what you asked me just now. 'What are you thinking, John?' I said.

" 'About the tree,' he said.

" 'It's so beautiful.'

" 'Yes, beautiful,' he said. 'Let's try to remember it,

Elly. All our lives. In winter, when it's black and frozen; when our own hearts are frozen and our faith is weak. Let's remember it then. Let's remember it always.' "

Eleanor paused.

"I remember it," she said. . . . "And I remember how, for a while, he sat there looking up at the blossoms in the moonlight, and that suddenly I knew he was praying. 'We ask it in the name of Jesus Christ,' he said, 'Who His own self bore our sins in His own body on the tree.' "

She paused again. Her eyes moved from the dead tree to the dying fire.

"He was never a happy man, Frank," she said.

"He's always felt too deeply to be happy."

"Yes—felt too deeply. Struggled too deeply. Even back there he was different from other young men; from the other divinity students. Half the time I had the feeling that he didn't want to be a minister at all. That he was somehow forcing himself to it."

"Because of what happened in that football game?"

"That was part of it, of course. But not all. Even without that I think something else would have made him do what he did. Not something outside him. Something inside."

She was sitting motionless beside me. Her eyes were dark in the flickering firelight.

"You've been his friend, Frank," she went on. "He's talked to you. You know how much he asks of himself—how deeply he looks into himself—how close he often came to darkness and despair. Do you remember how he sometimes talked about faith as being another dimension? He needed that dimension so terribly. And it never came to him easily. He had always to struggle for it, search for it.

"To search. . . . Sometimes I think that has been the whole of his life. It was why he became a minister. And why he came to China. For most of the others the usual things were enough: a pleasant parish, weddings and sermons, advice and comfort. But not for John. For him it had to be China: so poor, so wretched, so full of darkness. Search and faith—they were the same thing. To find light in that darkness. To make a dead tree bloom again, or a garden grow from a desert.

"I said he was never a happy man. That isn't true. I think there were times when he was happy. In his work. In those he loved. . . . Most of all, in Jean. . . . This may seem a strange thing to say, but Jean was more than a daughter to him; more than *his own* daughter. She was a child. Every child. She was life renewed; hope and faith renewed. . . ."

A tremor passed through her.

"When Jean died," she said, "all she had been to him died with her. And by then the rest was dead too. He had seen the failure of Christianity in China. He had seen what the Communists brought in its place. All he had believed in and lived by was gone and dead, and there was nothing to take its place. In Sanchow, in those last days, we were getting ready to leave, and I assumed that we'd be going back to the coast; maybe even to America. But when I spoke to him he shook his head. 'To what?' he said. 'Where will we go then?' I asked. 'To the west,' he said. 'West to what?' 'To the desert.'

"So we came," she said. "And I think he was right; that it was the only place to which he could have come. To the desert. To a world that was empty and naked and lost. As he was. He had to go on; always farther, always deeper. To Ningsia. To Borba. And now—"

"Now to where, Elly?" I said.

She looked at me for a long moment, and then she understood what I meant.

She shook her head slowly.

"No," she said. "No. He's alive, Frank. John's alive. I know it."

I started to speak again, but she went on softly, gently: "I know it, because I know that he *has* to live. That's the incredible thing. The miraculous thing. That all the rest is dead—but not he. I know it, because of a thing that happened on the night before he left Borba. . . . I haven't told you this before; I don't know why. Perhaps because until now I haven't been certain what it meant. . . . Anyhow, we were in the house, in the sitting room, and for hours he had been there in his chair by the window, as he always was, looking out into the darkness, listening to the wind. Then I got up and went out to the kitchen and was gone a while, and when I came back he was still there, but now he was no longer looking out or listening. He was doing something he hadn't done in months; almost since Jean died and we left Sanchow.

He was reading his Bible. . . . And I walked over and stood beside him, and suddenly the tears were streaming from my eyes, and I wanted to fall on my knees and give thanks to God. But instead I just stood there watching him, and then I said, 'Read it aloud, John. The way you used to.'

"So he read, and it was from Job, and he had read it often before: *Canst thou by searching find out God? Canst thou find out the Almighty unto perfection?*

"And then the answer: *It is as high as heaven; what canst thou do? Deeper than hell; what canst thou know?*"

A few minutes passed before she spoke again. Then she said:

"That's how I know, Frank. I may not have known then, but I know now. That all the rest may be dead, but not he. That he must go on living, go on searching. That that is what he is doing here—now; searching, as he has always searched —"

She didn't finish.

"For God, Elly?"

"For whatever it is," she said, "that is beyond the Black Sands."

We sat for a long while then, without speaking. The fire went out; it grew colder; but still we sat in front of the tents, side by side, in the darkness.

Beyond the Black Sands, I thought. . . .

I raised my hand. There was no breath of wind. But I could hear the wind. Far out in the darkness, I heard it humming across the wasteland.

I raised my head. There was the ancient tree; beyond the tree the night; beyond the night the stars. With the fire gone, they were brighter than before. Brightest of all was the great star I had watched before, burning white and pure above the desert to the north.

SIXTEEN

Toward morning the wind returned. It rose steadily until it was a howling tide, and again we spent a day in camp. One of the ponies was in bad shape, the sores on its legs having swollen into great abscesses. We did what we could for it, but it wasn't much.

The next day we moved on again. The wind was still blowing, but not so strongly, and we managed to breast it, hunched in our capes and hoods. We had repacked the ponies, so that the one with the bad legs had scarcely any load; but nevertheless, after an hour or so, it went down. Nothing we could do got it up again, and finally I had to shoot it. There was not a vulture, not a worm, not an ant in all the miles around us. It would probably lie there until the earth itself rotted away.

We did no more than ten miles that day . . . But what was a mile? What was a day?

Camp. Night. Wind.

The next day, as we were riding, a thought came to me out of nowhere. It was the sixth of September and my mother's seventieth birthday. I tried to visualize her in her house in Croton-on-Hudson. Going on from there, I tried to visualize New York, Shanghai, Korea, the front page of a morning newspaper. I might as well have been trying to see the far side of Uranus.

We made another ten miles, more or less. Our food and water were about half gone, and it was obvious that we had better get there soon.

There? I thought.

Where?

I remember sitting in my tent that night and beginning a letter to my mother. I remember the pencil breaking and my reaching for a knife to sharpen it; and perhaps I did sharpen it. But I didn't write any more. Instead, after a while, I got up and went to Eleanor's tent and sat down beside her as she lay between her blankets.

"We're almost there," I told her. "We'll be there tomorrow."

By sunrise we were off again.

"Seven," said Khitai.

"Half past seven."

"Eight."

(He never missed.)

As the morning passed, the wind dropped. The sun blazed on the black sand, almost as blindingly as if it had been snow. I rode with eyes closed, half-dozing, and let my pony pick its own way among the mounds and hollows.

Then something happened.

The pony stopped, I heard Khitai's voice, and opening my eyes, I saw what they saw: a trail of hoofprints and dried dung. It slanted in from our right— from the east—and stretched on before us, due north, in a course almost identical to our own. It was obvious from the dung-heaps that it had been made not long before, and I raised my eyes to the horizon ahead. But there was no hint of movement, nor even a cloud of dust against the sky.

The lamas' caravan? Or Bickel? Or both? The questions crowded into my torpid brain, found no answers, and trickled away like water into the sand. . . . All right, there was a trail. . . . We followed it.

But the day passed and still we found nothing, and when darkness came we pitched our tents close by the trail, in the lee of a black weathered mound. As usual, we ate almost in silence. We were now, we felt certain, within one short day's march of our objective, and by every normal standard should have felt anticipation and excitement—or at least apprehension; but apparently Eleanor, no more than I, was any longer capable of such emotion. By this stage of the journey even Khitai was subdued. No human being—man or woman or boy of twelve—could have kept his hope and strength alive in that world of desolation that encompassed us.

When he had gone to bed, Eleanor and I again sat in the darkness before the tents. At intervals we talked a little—less, I think, because we had anything to say than because we each needed to hear the sound of a living voice. I estimated that if we started at dawn we could reach the site of Karakorum by late afternoon. She expressed the hope that John was at least not alone, but had joined up, during his journey, with the mysterious caravan that had preceded us. Neither of us spoke of what was uppermost in our minds: that it was inconceivable that there could be living beings other than ourselves in this terrible immensity of silence and emptiness.

Again that night I awakened in the darkness. Again the wind was blowing, and from behind the wind, as once before, there seemed to come to me the faint pervading sound of shifting sands; the beat of a deep and distant rhythm as the wind moved across the sands. But when I lifted the tent-flap and stepped outside there was only the night and the stars and the dim shapes of the ponies shifting on their tethers.

Toward daylight the wind grew stronger, and by the time we set out it was pouring in a gale from the north. The sting of blowing sand was almost unendurable. The hair of the ponies had begun to fall out in tufts, and great green sores grew quickly on the bare places of their bodies. Sores had developed also on my own face and arms, but so complete was my lassitude that I scarcely noticed them. The world about us was shrouded and remote, and all that existed between heaven and earth was wind and sand and the black twisted rocks, moulded by centuries. We crawled on through the hours, until at last even our motion seemed an illusion. We ourselves, our identities, the breathing of our lungs and the pumping of our hearts, were no longer realities but the fabrications of our own numbed and fevered minds.

On that last day, however, we were not stopping. For anything. The ponies stumbled ahead. The faint trail led on, and we followed it.

And then another thing happened.

It was a thing, I am sure, that had been happening gradually, through the hours, but my awareness of it was abrupt—almost instantaneous. The wind had been howling. Now it had stopped. The sound in my ears was no longer of its violence but of immense and absolute stillness; the dark veils of sand had blown away, and the earth around us lay transfixed and frozen under an empty sky. Then I saw something else. The sand was gone from the earth as well. The dark choking drifts had vanished; mound, ridge and hollow spread naked to the horizon; still black, but with the blackness of rock, of iron, an endless sweep of hardness, of coldness, of unimaginable desolation, no longer a part of the living earth at all, but the surface of a burnt-out star.

And now, as I watched it, something of the same sort seemed to be happening to my own mind. Its fever was gone. Its shrouded torpor was gone. Like the earth itself, it was stripped and naked; the wind had scoured it, the sun had burned it clean; and I thought, yes, now finally you are seeing clear, perceiving clear, beyond the journey to journey's end, beyond illusion to reality. Here is the world ripped bare—its greenness gone, its softness gone, even its veil of sand gone—its bones, its skull, its carcass revealed at last. And here, too, is yourself laid bare, revealed—beyond hope, beyond fear, beyond illusion —in all your emptiness, your meaninglessness, your nothingness. Here is the sea to which all rivers flow, the waste in which all winds die. Here is the end. The answer. The truth. . . .

Then I looked up.

I looked up and I saw it. You may say it was a mirage, an hallucination, the trick of a fevered brain. But I say that I saw it. . . . *The star.* . . . It was full day. Above the black earth the sky glared like brass. But there it was: the great star I had watched in the blackness of the desert nights; alone, above the horizon to the north; faint but gleaming in the gulfs of space. And watching it now, I did a thing I had not done since I was a child. I prayed. I prayed the only prayer I knew:

Our father Who art in heaven,
Hallowed be Thy name. . . .

My pony stumbled, and I caught him up. Its hooves scraped thinly on an outcropping of rock.

Thy kingdom come,

Thy will be done. . . .

I looked around, and that was all there was. Bare rock. The wasteland. The sands were behind us; we had come beyond them. "I must find," John Bickel had said, "what is beyond the Black Sands."

I looked ahead again. At the waste. At the star. *Thy will be done. . . .*

We crept on.

And by midafternoon there was another change. The star had faded. The stillness was flawed. Deep within the stillness was the familiar sound—the sound of the wind; and although no wisp of it touched the barrens around us, I could hear it humming and moaning as it moved through the upper air. Perhaps three hours remained until dusk, but at the same time I grew aware of a shadow on the horizon to the north. As we moved on, the shadow deepened; it became a band of darkness; and then the band of darkness became a great escarpment, stretching across the earth before us as far as the eye could see.

It was this escarpment, I saw, that was protecting us from the wind. And from the sand as well. We had not passed beyond the wind, or the sands, but had merely been sheltered from them by the vast ridge of rock to the north; and now, above the crest of the ridge, I could see wave upon wave of blowing darkness, streaming across the empty sky. The sand seemed to hang poised for an instant over the summit and then sifted slowly down over the rocks of the escarpment, while the wind poured on overhead. Under the wind, under the rocks and sand, the earth lay before us in black frozen stillness.

I remember stopping. I remember glancing at my compass and then riding over to Khitai and looking at the watch on his wrist. But what I did was mechanical and meaningless. For as surely as if I had made it a hundred times before, I knew that our journey had reached its end. That beyond the great ridge lay the ruins of Karakorum.

My eyes went to Eleanor, but her face was hidden by her hood. And after a moment we moved on again. A few miles remained to the actual base of the cliffs, and for another hour or more we moved slowly toward them across the mounds and hollows, still following the caravan trail that wound faintly before us. As we rode, the light began fading from the sky. It was obviously too late to try to find a route that day up, or through, the escarpment, and near the first steep rocks we stopped and once again pitched our tents. Eleanor, I saw, was close to exhaustion. As soon as her tent was up she crept inside, and when, a few minutes later, I looked in at her, she seemed already asleep. Khitai too, as soon as he had tethered the ponies, wrapped himself in a blanket and lay still. Left alone, I sat on a boulder in front of the tents.

Start getting supper, I thought. . . .

But I didn't start. I didn't move. For a long time I sat motionless, watching the day drain from the sky, feeling the torpor flow, slow and deep, through every bone and cell of my body. . . . So we are there, I thought. The journey is behind us. We are *there*. . . .

I looked up. I looked at the black rock, the walls of the escarpment, the walls rising bare and forlorn into the twilight, and at their top the black sands streaming in veils across the sky. I looked for the star —the great star—the daylight star. But it was gone. Perhaps the escarpment hid it; or the blowing sand. Or perhaps I had never seen it. Only imagined it. Only conjured it up out of an exhausted and fevered brain; out of emptiness; out of nothingness.

The wind keened, thin and high.

And then it was no longer upward that I was looking, but at the earth around me. At the faint trail that led past our tents, bore on toward the black cliffs and veered to the right along their base. At the low mound of earth that cut it from view. At the thin thread of smoke that, as I watched, rose from behind the mound against the darkening sky. . . .

A minute passed. Perhaps longer. Then I got up, went into my tent and took one of the two Mausers. Carrying it, I followed the trail toward the cliffs, turned right, flanked the mound, and came out on the rim of a small crater-like hollow. On the floor of the hollow stood a single yurt. There were no camels, no ponies, no men or signs of men. Nothing moved except the thread of smoke twining up from the yurt into the dusk.

SEVENTEEN

I stood motionless, watching. I waited. But still nothing moved in the hollow below me. Then, holding the gun ready, I slowly descended. I reached the floor of the hollow, crossed it, approached the yurt and stopped. I listened, but there was no sound. Then I called out in Chinese:

"Who is here?"

My voice hung in the air. For a moment it seemed suspended above me like an almost palpable thing; then it faded, spiralled upward, became a part of the wind. Again there was only the wind—and the soft sound of my breathing.

I waited.

Then I reached for the tent flap, lifted it and entered.

The interior of the tent flickered in a faint yellow glow. There was heavy carpeting underfoot, and other carpets, of rich and intricate pattern, hung from the circular walls. On the far side of the tent, facing me, was a lama. He was sitting cross-legged among many cushions, dressed in a robe of yellow silk and wearing the yellow pointed hat of his priesthood. On the carpet before him stood a small prayer wheel that gave off thin tinkling sounds as he turned it gently with his hand. And to one side, against the wall, was an iron brazier that provided the flickering light, its smoke rising slowly and going out through a round hole in the roof. There was, I thought, an odor in the tent—a queer furtive little odor—but whether or not it came from the brazier I couldn't tell. It might have been the odor of incense, or of decay.

I stood for a moment within the entrance, but the lama gave no sign that he was aware of my presence. He was an old man—incredibly, fragilely old, with an age that seemed less human than reptilian—and the skin of his cheeks and forehead was stretched silk-thin across the bones. His mouth was a line without lips, his eyes deep crevices, in the bottom of which there was an occasional faint gleam, as of dark water. The hand turning the prayer wheel was fleshless and purple, like the claw of an ancient bird.

At last, as I moved closer, he raised his hand and looked up at me. Then he spoke, but in a language I could not understand.

"I know only Chinese," I said. "Do you speak Chinese?"

"I asked that you put down your gun," said the lama.

I hesitated.

"You will put down your gun, please. In this place no gun is needed."

His voice was low and rhythmical, the merest strand of sound in the dim stillness of the tent.

I leaned the Mauser against the carpeted wall. Then I turned back to him. "Where are the others?" I asked.

"The others?"

"The rest of your caravan. You came here with a caravan, didn't you?"

"Yes."

"Where are they? Where have they gone?"

"They have gone on to Karakorum."

Again he extended his hand and touched the prayer wheel, so that it tinkled softly. When it stopped I could hear, through the thick walls, the faint humming of the wind.

"And you—" I said "—why haven't you gone on with them?"

"Because I am very old," the lama answered. "And very tired. I should only have delayed the others by trying to cross the escarpment, and that I did not wish to do. Instead, as you see, I have put on my ceremonial robes; I have stayed here to meditate and pray a little; and soon now I shall die." Something that was almost a smile touched the seamed mask of his face. "It is not given to every man," he murmured, "to reach the end of his quest."

"Quest?" I repeated. "What quest? Why have you come here?"

For a moment the old eyes closed. Then they opened again—seemed to fix on me. "Perhaps it would be better," he said, "if you first answered that question."

"I am looking for a friend. A man who is lost. . . . Have you seen a man who was lost?"

"No, I have seen no one lost."

"Anyone, then? A man alone. A white man."

"I have seen John Bickel, if that is whom you mean."

My hands went tight. My heart was pounding. "When?" I demanded. "Where?"

"Mr. Bickel has traveled with us for many days."

"Where is he now?"

"He has gone on with the others to Karakorum."

"How long is it since they left here?"

"It is now perhaps a few hours." The old man paused. "But that does not matter," he said. "Time means nothing here."

I turned instinctively—to reach for the gun, to run from the tent. But even as I moved, something stopped me. It was not the lama's voice, for he did not speak. Perhaps it was the old eyes, silently watching me.

Instead, I took a step toward him. In the dim light I stood close before him, and when I spoke again my voice was as low as his. "Holy Father," I said, "you must help me. This man is my friend. He is in trouble, and I am searching for him. His wife and I have been searching for him over many weeks, many miles. And we must find him. . . . Help us, Father. Tell us what you know. . . . Why has he come here? Why did he join you? Why has he gone on to Karakorum?"

There was stillness in the tent. The lama neither spoke nor moved.

"Answer me," I pleaded.

"You are being answered, my son," he said. "Listen, and you will hear it."

Stillness again. And beyond the stillness the faint murmuring of the night.

"Do you hear it?" asked the lama.

"I hear the wind."

"Yes, of course—the wind. All men can hear it if they stop and listen. Only some more clearly than others." The voice dwindled, stopped—then resumed again. "That is why your friend has come here. Why I have come here. Why you too, though perhaps you do not know it, have come here. . . . Because we have heard the wind. Because we have heard the Black Sands blowing. . . ."

I stood motionless before him. I was staring as if hypnotized into the expressionless mask of his face.

"You have heard them, haven't you?" he said.

"Yes."

"You hear them now?"

"Yes."

"But you do not know what they mean?"

"No."

"Or what lies behind them?"

"No."

"You will know presently. All men will know presently."

"What will they know?"

Our words were a whisper. A whispered litany. My voice seemed no longer my own, but that of another standing beside me. . . .

And then, suddenly, my own again. My blood was pounding again. I heard my heart in the stillness, and then my voice, strained and rasping.

"What will they know?" I repeated. "For the love of God, what do *you* know?"

The sunken eyes gleamed faintly in the yellow light. The old man reached out and touched his prayer wheel, and when he spoke again the sound was as thin and delicate as a strand of silk.

"I know only a little, my son. And my desire to know more is not going to be gratified. But that little, for what it is worth, I shall tell you."

He paused. The wheel tinkled.

"You have of course heard of the Dalai Lamas?" he said.

"Yes."

"For us of the Buddhist faith the Dalai Lamas have for centuries been the incarnation of godhead upon the earth. Twelve years ago the then Dalai Lama died, and it became the duty of the Yellow Priests to search for his successor—for the newborn child whom the Maker and Destroyer of All Things would designate as his chosen one. I was one of those priests. In my search for the holy child I journeyed the length and breadth of Tibet. But I found no such child. Nor did anyone."

"But there is—"

"Yes, there is now in Lhassa a boy who is called by the name of Dalai Lama. But he is no true Dalai Lama. He is a substitute who was chosen when no true one was found; an expediency to delude men into believing that things are as they have always been. Most of the priests connived at this fraud. In a world without faith and soul, they were willing to defile even the most holy for the sake of pretense and power.

"And you have seen what has happened," said the old man. "He is a tool of power, a pawn of power; and that is all. From the north and east have come the dark hordes—the new barbarians—destroying the old temples, the old faiths, the deep wells from which the life of man's spirit is drawn. What remains is a shell, a few outward forms. And in the Potala, in Lhassa, the void at the heart of the shell. Not a high priest, but a political puppet. A living lie. A god of the godless.

"The venal and ignorant have accepted him. But there are some who have not; who can still tell the lie from the truth and have continued to seek for the true Dalai Lama. And I am one of them. For twelve years I have continued my search. I have followed the great trails of Asia from the Mekong to the Oxus, from Urga to Kandy, from Sind to Himachal; I have gazed into the bottomless waters of the sacred lakes of Ramthang; I have waited for the sign among the gorges of the Brahamaputra, in the dark swamps of Tsaidam and on the blue glaciers of the Tien Shan Mountains; I have meditated in the lost jungle shrines of Cambodia and the caves of the hermit monks in the farthest Hindu Kush. I am, as you can perceive, a very old man, but it has been the sustaining hope of my life that I might find the new and true Dalai Lama before I died."

"That search is what brought you here?"

"Yes."

"And you believe you will find him here?"

"No. Until recently I believed it—but no longer. Now I know that I shall find him nowhere." The priest closed his eyes again. "Now I know," he said, "that it is another child who has been born."

"Another child?"

"A child has been born—yes—born in the darkness beyond the wasteland. It is the child chosen by God: that is plain. But it is not the Dalai Lama. With the birth of this child there will be no Dalai Lama."

In the tent was stillness. Beyond the tent was the wind.

"I do not understand you," I said.

Once more the old eyes came slowly open. "I shall tell you one of the ancient legends of Asia," said the thin thread of voice. "It is a legend of the Great Khan Genghis, whom men called the Mighty Manslayer, the Master of Thrones and Crowns, the Emperor of All Men, and the Scourge of God. It was originally recorded by the great Mongol sage, Tenegri Tandor, and has been handed down through the centuries by the scholars and priests of our race. I first heard it when I was a young man, serving my novitiate in the Monastery of the Yellow Monks at Kharta Pu. It is called the Legend of the Black Sands.

"Eight hundred years ago, the story tells, vast storms of wind and sand arose in the region between the Altai Mountains and the Gobi Desert. The nomad tribes, terrified by these portents of nature, consulted the seers and wizards as to their meaning and were told that the storms announced the birth of a child who had been chosen by God to conquer the world. This child, they said, would, in the fulness of maturity, emerge from behind the sands. He would march, irresistible, to the north, the south, the east, the west, until he was master of the earth from sea to sea. He would march out of the desert, out of the heart of Asia, bearing the wrath of God against the evil of the world; and so great was this wrath, so terrible was its destruction, that it would slay his enemies unto the last man and turn the earth they inhabited into a waste of black sand."

The old man paused and touched his prayer wheel. "In all these things," he went on, "the seers and wizards were right. And they were right in another thing also. They said that this child would be recognizable at its birth by a mark which God would put upon it: a clot of blood held tightly in its hand. Genghis Khan was born holding such a clot. He was born in the valley beyond this ridge, during the Year of the

Swine in the Calendar of the Twelve Beasts, while the sands blew out from Karakorum across the waiting world."

His hand dropped from the wheel, and he contemplated it as if in a trance. "Do you begin to understand me now?" he asked.

I stared at him, but did not move nor speak. His head, under the tall hat, had begun to nod, gently and rhythmically. He seemed on the verge of sleep.

"Now eight hundred years have passed," he murmured, "and now the sands blow again. Now another child is born in the city beyond the sands—a child chosen by God—but not to be Dalai Lama. *For this child, too, holds in its hand a clot of blood. . . .*"

Once more the lids had closed over the ancient eyes; he sat unmoving, his head bowed, as if the effort of speech had exhausted him utterly. His face, in the flickering light, was appalling, unhuman. It was old not as the face of a man is old, but as a tree, a rock, the sand of the desert, with a terrible ageless majesty and calm. The moments passed and I stood watching him, and as I watched I heard the humming of the wind outside. It was still low, but seemed closer than before, and within it was the sound of sand flowing against the walls and roof of the tent. Through the hole in the roof black grains sifted down into the dim glow of the brazier.

That was all there was in the world: the wind and the sand. All there was inside of me: humming, revolving. . . .

And beyond them the yellow mask of the lama.

I heard myself speaking. "Do you ask me to believe—?"

The mask's eyes reopened. "I do not ask anything," said its voice. "It is not to be expected that a man of the West should understand the heart and mind of the East. You come from a world in which men accept as truth only what they are able to perceive with their external senses; in which the inward eye has been blinded by disuse; in which the realities of life and death have been replaced by the mindless charade you call civilization. I do not ask you to be what you are not. I merely remind you that there are in the world other realities and other truths than your own."

The prayer wheel tinkled. The dark sand drifted down onto the brazier.

"This child—" I said. "What is it that you prophesy for him?"

The lama shook his head slowly. "I am not a prophet. I am merely an old man, the priest of an ancient faith, who has read a little in the Book of Years. Eight centuries ago a wind blew over the sands of Asia, and a child was born who had been marked by God. He was born into an age in which the spirit of man had been sickened and died. China and Islam were fat with wealth and power, but the fire that had kindled them into greatness had been extinguished. The nations of Europe, although still professing Christianity, had forgotten the teachings of their messiah and were steeped in the ignorance and bloodshed of the Dark Ages. It was the destiny of this child to conquer and purge the world before the world should destroy itself." He paused, and again the claw of his hand reached out to the prayer wheel. "Now the great wind is blowing again; the world is sick again, dying again; and into it a child has been born again. Another child marked by God. . . ."

He was silent. The wheel tinkled and stopped. Beyond the walls of the tent the sound of the wind was louder.

"I do not know what name this child will bear," said the lama. "Nor how he will manifest himself to us. Perhaps it will be, like Genghis, as a conqueror leading armies; perhaps incorporeal and unseen, moving only in the stillness within the hearts of men. It does not matter. The child has been born. He exists. Slowly the Black Sands will drift out from this place across the world, and men everywhere will look up from the desert of the world, from the bleak and sterile waste they have made of the world, and know his presence. And they will know, too, that there can be no evading him, no turning back from him—just as there can be no turning back for us who have come to find him."

It seemed to me that I had ceased to breathe and that my heart was no longer beating; all that was left to me was a dim consciousness, transfixed and imprisoned. I struggled to break from the prison.

"I have come to find John Bickel," I said.

The words were as if wrenched from my flesh. But

they were no more than a whisper. They hung in the stillness, became a part of the stillness, part of the whispering sand. For now the sand seemed to be pouring in a dark tide through the hole in the roof. It poured down onto the brazier; soon it would cover the brazier; soon the glow would be gone. All that was left of it was a faint fading gleam in the eyes that were watching me.

"Yes, of course," said the soft voice. "To find your friend; the friend you once knew. And if you find him, my son—then what will you do?"

"I shall bring him back."

"Back to what?"

"To the world. To life."

The old head shook slowly. . . . Or was it the walls of the tent that were moving? As I watched now, they seemed to be gently revolving around the squatting figure before me. . . . The wind had swelled to a deep moaning. Through it the lama's words fell slow and measured, like drops of water in a cave.

"No, my son," said the voice, "you will not bring him back. He cannot go back. He has gone too far ever to return to the world from which he came. It is a long journey that he has made—longer than most men's—and he has seen farther than most men. He cannot go back; he can only go on. To whatever lies beyond the sands. Into the darkness. Into the future."

The wind was louder. The light of the brazier was out.

"That is all you see in the future? Darkness?"

"What I see in the future is the past. I see men killing and dying, and darkness everywhere, trickling down into the forlorn temples of gods without worshippers and beliefs without believers; in the dead bodies of men lying in streets and fields; in the hearts of men still living; in the black waste of the desert and the black waste of the bombs. I see the sands blowing across the waste—as they have blown before—as they must always blow when the soul of man is sick and dying. I see their shadow upon the earth, the shadow of ancient prophecy. And dimly—very dimly, for my eyes are old and the light is gone—I see beyond the shadow that which in the end will pierce the shadow. The shape of a world that is making, of a future that is coming, of new life that is born. . . ."

The voice faded and was gone. The aged face was gone. I was suddenly alone in the tent: alone with the revolving walls, the pouring sand, the sound of the wind. The wind rose wildly, seemed to enter the tent, closed in upon me, howling. As on that night in Borba, it was no longer a thing outside myself, but within me, a part of me. In my heart and brain. In my bones and blood.

I stumbled. I put out my hand. I was trying to call out something. Perhaps it was "John! John!"

Then there was stillness. Blackness.

EIGHTEEN

"John—"

No answer.

"John—"

"It's I, Frank," said a quiet voice.

I opened my eyes, and Eleanor was bending over me. I was lying in my tent. The flap was pulled back and outside it was daylight.

"Elly, I've found out—that John—"

"Yes, I know," she said.

"You know?"

"You told me last night. When you came back."

"When I—" I struggled to remember, but there

was only darkness. And deep within the darkness, a face and a voice.

"You had fever," said Eleanor. "A high fever." Her hand was on my forehead. "I think it's gone now."

I lay still for a moment. Her hand felt soft and cool.

"The wind's gone too," I said.

"Yes, the wind has dropped."

Abruptly I sat up. "We'd better start," I said. "He can't be far, Elly. The old man said—"

"We'll start later. First you must rest a while."

"I've rested all night."

But when I tried to get to my feet my head spun gently—the tent began to spin—and I lay back again.

"We'll go in a while," said Eleanor. "When you're stronger."

"But John—he's there, up ahead—and we must—"

"Yes, soon. After you've slept again."

A sudden anger filled me. At my weakness, my impotence. "Damn it, Elly, we're almost there," I said. "I can't hold us up now—can't do this to you—"

But she was no longer listening. "Here, I've brought you these," she told me. From beside her she produced a bottle of tablets and a cup of broth, and she sat beside me while I took them.

"When you've slept again you'll feel better," she said, and after a few moments left the tent.

"Get up. Get up," I told myself.

But I didn't get up.

A little later Khitai put his head in through the flap. "You are feeling better, sir?" he asked.

"Yes—better."

"I thought you might like to know the time, sir." He consulted my watch, on his wrist. "It is now exactly eight forty-seven and fifteen seconds."

Then I must have slept again.

When I next awoke I was alone in the tent. My body felt empty, drained, but my head was clear, and when I sat up it did not spin. Moving slowly, I crawled to the flap, opened it and went out.

Judging from the sun, it was almost noon. The sky was cloudless and windless. On three sides the waste spread away, black and frozen, and on the fourth the ridge rose like a wall of iron. Eleanor and Khitai were squatting beside a small dung fire, and I joined them, but did not sit down.

"I'm ready," I announced.

"It's too soon," said Eleanor. "Rest some more, and if you're all right later—"

"I'm all right now."

She made me sit down. She felt my forehead again and took my pulse. Then she brought me a plate of food and sat by while I forced myself to eat it.

"I've been thinking, Frank—" she said. "If the caravan is only a few hours ahead, Khitai and I can go on, while you stay here, and—"

"No," I said.

"Then we'll wait until tomorrow."

"No."

There was more argument, I think. I don't remember. But it was one argument of my life I was resolved I was going to win. Presently we were striking the tents, packing the gear, loading the ponies. And when we had finished Eleanor was standing beside me and looking up into my face.

"Frank," she murmured, "I can't tell you—"

"Don't," I said.

Then we mounted our ponies. We followed the faint trail toward the base of the cliffs, turned right, flanked the low mound that rose before us, and came out on the rim of the small crater-like hollow. The hollow was empty. Its floor was a smooth sweep of black sand. My eyes went to Eleanor—to Khitai—but they were both watching the trail ahead.

Skirting the hollow, we rode on.

The trail climbed, dipped, twisted, climbed again. Sometimes it seemed almost to peter out among the flinty rocks; but always it resumed again, led on again, and at intervals we came to the deep gouges of hoofprints, where the camels of the caravan had struggled for footing in the sloping sand. Scarcely any of the prints were as yet drifted over. The animal droppings which appeared now and then were obviously not more than a day old.

The dips were fewer than the rises. Slowly we gained height. And presently, looking up, I saw that we were no longer skirting the cliffs, but had penetrated them. Walls of rock now loomed on either side. We had come to a pass through the escarpment.

Through—or over. For the trail was not level, but, on the contrary, climbed even more steeply than before, boring on and up like a slanting tunnel in the rock. Gradually the sand fell away until there was only rock: rough and thrusting underfoot, rising sheer around us, all but shutting out the sky overhead. The ponies, already worn out from their long journey, slipped and stumbled among the boulders, and after a while we stopped, redistributed their loads and ourselves continued afoot.

"Frank, you can't—" Eleanor protested.

"Yes I can," I said.

And I could. . . . I bowed my head, bent forward and moved on. It was not strength that did it, for there was no strength left in me. It was simply numbness: the numbness of bone and blood, the numbness of dream. Through it, dimly, I could hear the scraping of feet. I could see my own feet moving beneath me. I counted a hundred steps. Another hundred. Then I lost track. I slipped, fell, picked myself up, moved on again. "It is now two-thirty, sir," Khitai's voice said behind me. And a while later: "It is three."

Then Eleanor fell. I neither saw nor heard it, but suddenly stumbled against her as she was struggling to rise to her feet. Her face was drawn, her breathing labored, and a streak of blood showed on her hand where she had struck it against an edge of rock.

We stopped and I bandaged it; then we moved on again. "It can't be far now," I told her.

Far to what?

It was I who asked the question; not she. Throughout the day she had asked not a single question. . . .

"You told me last night," she had said. . . . As I climbed now I tried to force my mind back into the darkness. *What* had I told her? How had I returned to our camp? What had happened? . . . But there was only darkness—darkness spinning, darkness humming— and beyond it a whisper and the ancient mask of a face.

The lama had been there. Then he had not been there. . . .

I counted a hundred steps.

Another hundred.

Then I was listening. It is the fever again, I thought: the fever spinning, humming, in your body and brain. . . . Or was it the wind again? . . . I looked up, and there was the deep gorge of the pass. There were the walls of the pass, rising black and desolate to their jagged ridges. Between the ridges the sky was streaked with long veils of blowing sand.

I counted sixty-three steps. I remember it: sixty-three. Then there was Eleanor again. This time she had not fallen, but simply stopped and sat down, and she was sitting motionless on a boulder, her head bent and her eyes on the ground.

"We'll rest here," I said.

And a while after:

"We'll camp here."

"No. No, Frank, I'm—"

"It's better," I said.

But there was no place level enough to pitch the tents.

I studied the pass above us. "It looks as if there's a spot up ahead," I told her. "I'll go and see. Then I'll come back and get you."

She murmured something in protest, but did not move. I told Khitai to watch the ponies. Then I climbed slowly up the trail. It rose steeply, leveled off somewhat—but not enough—then steepened again and twisted, and when I turned to look back the others were out of sight. Ahead, on the floor of the pass, the boulders rose, tier upon tier, in black tumbled confusion.

The track wound between them, and I followed it. In the dim light I could still see the level stretch which I thought I had spied out from below. If I was tired I didn't know it. If I was feverish I didn't know it. All I was aware of was an encompassing numbness—and beyond it the boulders and the wind. Now that I was alone, the wind seemed louder; no longer a humming but a high, thin wail, filling the air above. But on the floor of the pass, before me, was only black rock and stillness. There was no sound or movement of any kind.

And then, suddenly, there *was* a movement. At first it appeared to me that one of the boulders ahead had begun to sway, as if of its own imbalance, and was about to topple down upon me. But a few moments later, circling it, I came out on the flat stretch I had been seeking and saw that it was a crouching camel. Nearby were the shapes of other camels, almost indistinguishable from the great rocks among which they lay, and beyond them, half sheltered by an overhanging cliff, the dim outlines of three flat-topped yurts.

Now there was another sound in the stillness: the sound of the beating of my heart.

I saw something else move. There was a stirring of shadow within shadow, and a figure came toward me from the yurts. As it approached I saw that it was a squat leather-faced Mongol, dressed in the rough felt and wool of a desert tribesman.

"Where is the white man?" I asked.

He stared at me without answering.

"Where are the lamas?"

Still he said nothing, but after a moment turned and went back toward the yurts; and I followed him. At the entrance of the central yurt he stopped and said something I could not understand. Then he lifted the flap and went in. Whether he intended it I don't know—but I went in after him.

As in the other yurt the night before, the interior flickered with faint yellow light. Here, too, was an iron brazier, carpets underfoot, more carpeting on the walls. On the far side of the tent, however, was not one figure, but three. That was all they were: figures: not men. They were sitting motionless and crosslegged, as the old lama had sat, but I could distinguish nothing more, for the outlines of their bodies were concealed by thick robes and their faces by the shadow of tall conical hoods. I advanced halfway toward them and stopped, trying in the dimness to search out their features. And I could feel their eyes —though I could not see them—fixed on mine.

The man who had brought me in murmured something and stepped aside. The three figures said nothing.

"You are lamas?" I asked.

The numbness had returned—leaden, crushing. I could barely force myself to the effort of speech.

"Yes," said the figure in the center, "I am a lama."

"You are going to Karakorum?"

"Yes."

"Where is the white man who is with you?"

There was no answer.

"Where is the missionary, John Bickel?"

Still the lama didn't answer. In the dim light his pointed hood seemed to move slightly, as if he were looking in turn at the two figures beside him. But he spoke no word, and there was no further movement. The figure to his right was smaller than he, that to the left considerably taller. Or perhaps they were sitting on different levels; I could not be sure. In all other respects they appeared identical: robed, hooded, faceless.

I could not even see the eyes that were watching me.

"I am sorry," said the one in the center, "but we cannot help you."

"Yes you can. You know where he is."

"I am sorry."

"You know. . . . He is here with you. . . . And I demand . . ."

My voice rasped—thickened. The numbness thickened. Again, everything beyond it began slowly to revolve.

"You demand—?" said the figure.

"I demand . . . I mean, I beg of you . . ."

I closed my eyes. With all the will that remained to be I tried to wrench my mind back to control and clarity. You are too tired, I thought. You have come too far and are too tired. . . .

There was no sound now in the tent. Only the sound beyond it, growing louder. In another moment, I knew, I would fall.

Then there was a movement behind me. The tent flap had opened and someone had entered. Eleanor Bickel was standing beside me. She was standing motionless, facing the three hooded figures . . . then no longer motionless, but moving forward again, slowly . . . and as she moved, one of the figures moved too. It was not the figure who had spoken, but the one on the left, the tall one; and as Eleanor approached, he arose and came toward her. There was a low sound from her—not words, but merely a sound —like a hushed sob. There were two shadows standing close in the dim light.

Then only one shadow.

NINETEEN

I can recall almost nothing of those first incredible moments. I remember John Bickel's voice. I remember his coming closer and the light touching him and my first glimpse of his features under the folds of his hood. But what we did or said—or if we said anything —I do not know.

Then we had left the tent. We were moving away from it, past the crouching camels, John and Eleanor ahead, I a little behind; we had come to a sort of hollow among the boulders, and Khitai was there and he was speaking and Bickel answering; and then the Bickels had gone somewhere—behind the boulders, perhaps—and the boy was gone, and I was sitting by a black rock, alone, in the fading light. I was near to complete exhaustion. The shock of finding Bickel, which for an instant had quickened my mind into awareness, had passed as quickly as it had struck, leaving no exhilaration, no satisfaction, nothing. My body and brain alike seemed paralyzed, too spent to move or think or feel. So we had found Bickel. The search was over. . . . Well. . . . Grains of black sand sifted gently down the rocks and piled in little drifts against my feet.

When I opened my eyes it was almost dark. Eleanor was bending over me.

"Supper is ready, Frank," she said.

With an effort I got to my feet. Our tents, I saw, had been pitched among the boulders, and the ponies tethered close beyond. In front of the tents a small fire was going, with Khitai bending over it and Bickel sitting nearby. Approaching, I put my hand on his shoulder. That was all. I touched his shoulder once, lightly, and then sat down at a little distance. Khitai brought me a tin plate, and Eleanor gave one to her husband and sat beside him.

He was wearing a robe of some sort of rough homespun, but its hood was now thrown back, and in the firelight I saw clearly for the first time the man I had journeyed so long and far to find. The most striking thing about him, now as always, was his hair. Whatever hardship and agony he had endured in the two years since I had seen him, they had not thinned or faded that flaming crest. But the rest of him was almost unrecognizable; for now his beard, too, had grown, covering his jaw and chin, and his upper face, once broad and well-fleshed, seemed to consist only of cheekbones and eyes. The eyes, indeed, appeared enormous—like those of a starving man. They were neither dull nor feverish, however, but cool-gray and abstracted. When he raised them they seemed not to be looking at me at all but at something within or beyond me.

"I had scarcely thought we would meet again, Frank," he said quietly.

I forced myself to the effort of speech. "Thank God we've found you."

"Eleanor has told me how far you have come. And why. She has told me all you have done for her."

"It was nothing," I said.

"No, it was not nothing. It was a great deal. It was more than any friend—"

His voice trailed away. He was no longer looking at me. Bending to his plate, he ate with slow machine-like motions.

"And you, John," I said. "You're all right? You're not sick?"

"No, I am not sick," he answered.

"You're thin."

"Yes, I am thin. I had run out of food when I met the lamas, and they have little enough themselves."

"How long have you been with the lamas?"

"About ten days."

"We first heard about the lamas from another caravan," I said. "Then later we picked up the track."

"Eleanor has told me."

"Down at the foot of the pass I found the old lama. He told me you'd gone on, and we followed; but when I came into the tent I didn't recognize you. I thought I was speaking to three other lamas."

Bickel said nothing.

"You didn't know me either, did you?"

A moment passed before he answered. Then he said: "Yes, Frank, I knew you."

I cannot say that I felt surprise. I was beyond surprise, as beyond all emotion. But I know that I stared at him. "Then why—" I murmured "—why didn't you—"

"Because I didn't yet know that Eleanor was with you. Because I thought it better if—"

"If what?"

"If you did not find me," he said.

He was no longer looking at me, but into the fire, and his face, in its dim glow, was like a skeletal mask. I looked at Eleanor, sitting beside him. I searched her face for a sign of what I should say—or do—but she too was watching the fire and seemed unaware of my glance. And now I saw that her face was somehow different from before. It showed no animation, no trace of joy or exhilaration at being at last with her husband, but neither did it hold the anxiety and fear that had haunted it through the long weeks just past. There was calmness in it. There was—I fumbled for the word—acquiescence. What her husband had told her I of course did not know, but whatever it was she had understood it, accepted it.

Or was it, perhaps, what she had known in her heart from the beginning?

They did not speak. None of us spoke. The silence tightened around us, and I struggled to break out of it. It is preposterous, I thought. It is insane. You have come three thousand miles to find a man, and now at last you have found him and you have nothing to say to him. Or he to you. . . . Stand up now. Go to him. Talk to him. . . . He is your old friend. Talk as you used to talk. In Peiping, Chungking, Shanghai. In the neat living rooms, with the chintz at the windows, the sherry on the table, the organ in the corner.

Talk about what?

Handball?

Jean?

I didn't move. I couldn't move. I sat there among the boulders, in the black sand, and it was as if the sand were binding me fast to the earth. It was now full night, and the stars were out. In their dim light I could see the escarpment rising steep and black above us. High in the darkness I could hear the hum of the wind.

Khitai was standing before me.

"You have not eaten, sir," he said.

I shook my head.

"You do not wish to eat?"

"No."

Khitai took my plate and went back to the fire. Torpor was heavy in my brain; my eyes wanted to close. Around me, the fire, the three figures, the night and the stars began slowly to revolve.

With an almost violent act of will I jerked myself to my feet. I went over to Bickel.

"I'll get your things," I told him.

He looked up at me.

"From the lamas' caravan. You must have a pack, don't you?"

He nodded. "But there is no need—"

"It's best to do it now," I said. "We'll want an early start in the morning."

"An early start?"

"For the trip back. If we start at dawn we should be able—"

I stopped and looked at him. He looked at me. And he was shaking his head.

"I am not going back, Frank," he said quietly.

"Not going—"

"No."

"But then—" The words stuck on my tongue. "What are you saying?" I asked. "What will you do?"

"I shall go on with the lamas."

"Go on—where?"

"To Karakorum." Bickel paused and raised his eyes. "It is no longer far," he said. "It lies in the valley beyond this pass."

A long moment passed before I spoke again.

"Then it's true, John?" I said.

"What is true?"

"That that is why you left Borba. Why you are here."

"Yes."

"And these lamas: what have they to do with it?"

"As I told you, I met them about ten days ago—while I was crossing the Altai Mountains. My food had run out, and they fed me. And when I found that they were going where I was, I joined them."

"What do you mean," I said slowly, "by *joined them?*"

My eyes were fixed on his homespun robe, and for an instant he glanced down at it. Then he looked up again, and into my thoughts, and smiled faintly. "If you are asking if I have become a lama," he replied, "the answer is no, I have not."

"What have you become then? Why have you stayed with them? What are you doing with them?"

"Suppose we say that I am a fellow pilgrim."

There was a silence. Bickel stared into the fire, and his eyes glinted with its reflected light. Behind him the cliffs rose, dark and still, to the stars.

I realized that he was listening.

And I was listening too. I did not want to, but still I listened. And it was there. High in the darkness above us; filling the night; pouring thin and cold across the black walls of rock into the very crevices of body and brain.

Swiftly I crouched beside Bickel. "John—" I said. "Listen. You must listen. Not to that, but to me." There was urgency, almost desperation, in my voice.

"You're tired. Tireder than you know. You've been alone too long. . . . But now you're not alone. We're here, John—Eleanor and I. Here beside you. To help you—"

He did not seem to hear.

"John!" My fingers gripped his bony shoulder. "I know what you've been through. Believe me, I do. Eleanor has told me. Yeng has told me. I know what it's been for you. . . . But you can't go on with it. You must put it behind you. . . . You feel my hand, don't you? It's real, John. I'm real. Eleanor's real. And we're here. Here to help; to take you home."

He turned his head slowly.

"Home?" he said.

"Out of this place. Back to Borba. To the world."

His eyes fixed on mine.

"The world isn't home," he said gently. "Where I am going is home."

"John!"

Still I gripped him. Tight, trembling—and impotent. Still the words poured out; and they were only words. His mind is gone, I thought. This is not the John Bickel you knew. It is a shell—a shadow.

But Eleanor?

Again I looked at her, and she was sitting as before, her hands in her lap, her eyes on the fire.

"Elly—"

A moment passed before she spoke. Then she said quietly: "He must do what he has to do, Frank."

"Has to—"

"He must go on." She paused. "And I must go with him."

I stared at her. I started to speak again, but this time there were not even words. And then she had reached out and taken my hand and was continuing in her soft voice:

"You've done so much, Frank," she said. "So terribly much for us. But now that I've found John—now that I know at last why he has come here—I understand why he can't go back. And I can't go without him."

"What do you mean—can't?"

"We must go on to Karakorum. We must learn what has happened there."

There was the word again. . . . *Happened.* . . . For a moment it seemed to hang in the air between us. Then it was gone, and there was only the hum of the wind.

"Elly, for the love of God—"

There was a movement beside me, but it was not Eleanor. It was Bickel. He had turned his head and was looking at me, and in the faint light he again seemed almost to be smiling. "Yes, Frank," he said. "That is it. Perhaps that is all of it. *For the love of God.* . . .

The smile—if it had been a smile—faded. His gray eyes were fixed on mine.

"I am not mad, Frank," he said. "Believe me, I am not. Nor am I trying to destroy myself. It is not despair that has brought me to this place."

"What is it then?"

"Perhaps it is—hope."

His voice was low but clear. His eyes were clear. But behind them was a terrible burning intensity. . . . *Was* he mad? I didn't know. I no longer even knew what madness was. Or sanity. . . . We had journeyed beyond them into something deeper, something darker.

"Hope for what?" I said. My voice was no more than a whisper. "Why have you come here? What are you looking for?"

Bickel did not answer at once. Instead, he picked up a handful of sand and let it run slowly out through his fingers.

"You say you have seen the old lama," he said at last. "What did he tell you? Why did *he* say he had come here?"

"He said he had been looking for the new Dalai Lama."

"Go on."

"But that he had not found him—he would not find him—"

"Why wouldn't he find him?"

"Because—" I hesitated. In the darkness beyond the firelight I could see the ancient mask of a face. In the stillness I could hear the thin tinkling of a wheel. "Because he said—because the sands—" I struggled to pull myself together. "I don't know; I don't remember," I murmured. "I was sick. I had fever—"

"I think you do remember," said Bickel quietly. "What did he say then?"

"Then he told me what he called the Legend of the Black Sands.

"Which you did not believe?"

"Believe? Good God, man. . . . About Genghis Khan, a second child, a bloody hand. . . . Who could believe such things?"

"I could," said Bickel. "I do."

I tried to reach out: to touch him, to seize him. But I could not move. Bickel and Eleanor did not move either. We sat like stone figures in the night.

Then Bickel said:

"These things of which you speak are symbols. As a prayer wheel is a symbol. Or a star. Or a cross. Here in the land of Genghis they have been woven around the name of Genghis; but there is much more to the legend than that. In one form or another it appears in the traditions of almost every Eastern faith: of Buddhism and Taoism, of the cults of Brahma and Zoroaster, even in the ancient writings of the Asiatic Moslems and Christians. But the legend itself is older than any of the faiths into which it has been absorbed. It is as old as man and man's awareness of powers beyond himself. Since my first days in the East I have heard of it, read of it, tried to understand it; and though it has been altered to fit the pattern of many kings and conquerors, prophets and gods, the core of the legend remains always the same. It is the core of death and rebirth. Of a world that has sickened and must change or die."

He paused. His eyes were watching me.

"That is what the sands mean," he said. "Change.

. . . And, strangely, it is out of the desert—the un-changing desert—that change comes: *always*. It is the place of the past and the future, of endings and beginnings. Of the beginning of man himself, grop-ing up out of a prehistoric darkness. Of man's faiths and scourges; of Buddha, Krishna, Mohammed, Christ; of Attila, Tamerlane, Baber, Genghis. All these have been born of the desert—of the waste and the wil-derness—out of the emptiness of a world that *must* change. And out of the emptiness, before them, blows the great wind and the sands."

Again he paused. The eyes had not left my face.

"I see that you do not stop me, Frank," he said. "I see you are no longer quite convinced that you are listening to the ravings of a madman."

"I don't know," I murmured.

"Yes, you know. You know, because you too, in your own life, have known the Black Sands. In your conscious mind, perhaps, you have tried to ignore them; but they were there nevertheless—sifting deep into your heart and soul. You have heard the wind, and the sands blowing in the wind; you have heard them in the night and have been afraid and tried to pray."

I stared at him, motionless, and something cold and thin as a snake coiled slowly through my body.

"Yes, you have heard them," said Bickel. "You do not have to be a Mongol herdsman or a Tibetan priest, nor even a missionary who for a time lost his faith. All men have heard them—only some more clearly than others—and I think that you, Frank, have heard them very clearly indeed. . . . On your journeys about the world, perhaps; in the chancelleries, on the battlefields, in the cities and towns of China; in what you have seen and known and written; in your bed, when you are alone at night. . . . Yes, you have heard them, you have known them—you have felt the sickness of the world and the Black Sands blowing—and that is why you are here, why you have come to this place, to this wasteland, to this world beyond the world—because you too—as I, as all men —must find what lies beyond them. . . ."

There was a long silence. The fire was dying. Above us the walls of the pass rose, black and desolate, to the stars.

"The future," said Bickel. "That is what lies beyond them. The shape of the future. I do not know its shape; the lamas do not know it; no man knows it. But it is there. It is being born. It is not necessary that we see beyond the Black Sands to know that. We may know it from looking into our own hearts."

His voice was low but clear. His eyes looked past me into the black miles of the night. And now that was all there was between earth and sky—the voice, the eyes, the night—the eyes which saw in the night that which was not visible to others.

"The darkness does not lie before us," he said. "But behind. In the world we have left. Most of my life I have lived in that darkness. I have felt it within me, corroding, poisoning—the darkness of hatred, of violence, of evil—rising and swelling until, with my own hands, I once killed a fellow man. I have seen it around me: in men everywhere; in their savagery and ignorance, their lust and fear; in how they kill and die and what they make of the incomparable miracle of life. It was because I knew this darkness that I was a clergyman, a minister of God. I hoped that in some measure to bring His light into it; to hold back the night.

"But I failed. Neither more nor less than other men, I failed—because the night was too dark, too deep, and what I thought was the light of God was only the dim flickering of illusion. I have seen the illusion of our old faith: that men's souls could be saved by good works, by missions and hymnals and basketball courts; by words, words, words—but forgetting God. I have seen the illusion of a new faith that seeks to change the world—by denying God. I have seen the forgetters and the deniers and the realities behind their illusions: the realities of the bullet and the bomb, of hatred and fear, of struggle and death. We have withdrawn from God—not half the world, but all of it, all of us—and without God there is only death.

"I have seen it all," he said. "I have seen my daughter raped and killed by men whom I had loved and trusted. It is not only for her that I grieve, but for them; for all of us who have made ourselves and our world what they are. It is that world that is dying; that must die. The wind is blowing, the sands are drifting; soon it will be gone and in its place. . . ." He paused. The fire was out, and I could no longer see his face. . . . "In its place," he said, "will be the new world—the new life—the life that even now is being born in the darkness beyond the Sands of Karakorum."

My eyes strained into the night, but saw nothing. As if from the pit of a dream, I heard myself speaking. "But there is nothing there," I said "—in Karakorum. Only a ruin. Only a waste."

"Exactly. That is *why* it is being born there. Born in the waste—out of emptiness—because of emptiness—to fill the emptiness."

"—this child—"

"Yes."

"—who will change the world—"

"Yes."

"—because it holds in its hand—" My voice caught. My mind spun in darkness.

"*Because it holds in its hand,*" said Bickel softly, "*what the hearts of men are ready to receive.*"

TWENTY

He was silent. And I was silent too. How long we sat there in the night I do not know. At intervals wisps of wind and sand blew down the pass from the escarpment walls, making a soft hissing noise among the rocks. There was no other sound. Bickel sat motionless, his gaunt figure barely discernible against the blackness beyond. Beside him, motionless, sat Eleanor, her head bowed as if in prayer.

Finally Bickel stood up.

"So I must go on," he said, "to Karakorum."

"When?" I asked dully.

"When the lamas go on. They have stopped here

to rest and meditate, and when they are ready they will send for me."

Eleanor had risen too. She came toward me and stopped and, without speaking, bent her head and kissed me. Then she turned and took Bickel's hand and led him silently into her tent.

I remained sitting where I was. Khitai, too, had gone to his tent. I was alone. And yet not alone, for Bickel was still there—his figure, his eyes, his voice, they were there in the darkness beside me—his voice, low and clear, speaking out of the darkness, echoing in my brain—and I strove with all the strength that was in me, with all my will, with all my sanity, to think, to analyze, to reach decisions. But it was no use. The harder I tried, the less I succeeded; the tighter the web of darkness closed in upon my mind. I no longer seemed even to know why I was there, or what had happened—much less what was going to happen. Nor did I care. Thought and will were gone. Even fear was gone. Once again a monstrous numbness enveloped me—the numbness of night, the numbness of sand—until that was all there was on all the earth: the sand and the night, the wind behind the night. And myself a part of them, one with them. . . .

You are tired, I thought. You are feverish. You must sleep. You must sleep. . . .

I awoke to darkness and wind.

The wind was no longer humming high in the night, but was all around me: pouring down the black walls of the escarpment, moaning among the boulders and hollows of the pass. As I sat up, its edge bit into my lips and eyes. My legs and body were half buried in sand.

But there was something else, too, that had had a part in my awakening. Not only wind and sand, but something that had *happened*. I looked about me. Dimly, in the blowing darkness, I could see the three tents, the dead fire, the outlines of our ponies, heads down and hunched against the blast. Beyond them the pass climbed sharply upward toward its hidden summit.

That much I remember. And I remember the deathly cold that seemed to fill me as I stumbled the few yards to the center tent.

"John!" I called. "John!"

And then, "Elly!"

But there was no answer.

Fumbling in my clothes, I found my flashlight. I brought it out, snapped it on, pulled back the tent flap.

The tent was empty.

The beam fell on a shred of paper. Entering the tent, I crouched over it.

Goodbye, dear Frank, I read. *They have sent for us and we must go. I as well as John: you understand that, don't you? Without John there is no I. It is heartbreaking to leave Khitai, but we must. What is in the house in Borba is for him and Yeng. What is in our hearts is for the three of you. Eleanor.*

Turning, I ran to Khitai's kit. The boy was there, motionless and asleep. One arm was thrown out from under the blanket, and on the wrist I could see the glowing dial of my watch. As the light struck him he murmured and turned over; but he did not wake.

Then I was outside again. I was running again. My body was bent almost double against the blast of wind, my feet slipping and stumbling, the beam of the flashlight wobbling crazily over the boulders and sand. It was only a few yards to the sheltered platform where the lamas' caravan had been camped, and in a matter of seconds I was there. But the caravan was not. All that remained was a jumble of footprints, a few odds and ends of refuse, and the black sand sifting over them. On the far side of the platform a faint track led upward and disappeared among the boulders of the pass.

I remember standing motionless, staring. I remember the sound of the wind, and then another sound higher, wilder, than the wind—the sound of my own voice crying out. I ran forward, stumbled, fell. I lay prone on the rock and sand and my body was trembling, as with a paroxysm of fever.

Then I was up again—moving again. No longer running, no longer panting and stumbling, but following slowly and deliberately along the track: across the platform, up its farther side, between the boulders that rose into the darkness beyond. The fever was gone. The frenzy and the fear were gone. I felt nothing and was aware of nothing, except of the black rocks gliding past me and the wind blowing ever more violently into my face. My movements were less that of a man than of a machine, blind and predestinated; my consciousness narrowed to the next step, the next turning. It contained no shred of thought or will—of where I was going or what I would do—but was merely a driving mindless compulsion. This, at last, was the end: that was all I knew. This, whatever it might be, was the resolution of the nightmare.

I moved on. . . .

I do not know how long I struggled up the howling desolation of that pass. Now and then, peering ahead, I could see dimly the great walls of rock still tiering above me; then blackness closed in, wind and sand closed in, and they were gone. The sound of the wind had now swelled to an insane roar, a cataract of drumming echoing thunder that filled the air like the night itself. The very earth—the rocks, the boulders, the mass of the escarpment—seemed to be trembling deep in its hidden core.

The glint of my flashlight wavered feebly before me: the merest phosphorescent midge in a midnight ocean. Then it went out. The trail was gone. Everything was gone. Everything except the steep funnel of the pass, still rising and twisting into darkness. I climbed on: blind, numb, insensate. Most of the time, I think, I climbed with eyes closed. The lids shut out nothing except the searing waves of wind and sand.

I climbed on. Then I had stopped. Or had I fallen? I was lying sprawled across a knob of rock, my eyes still closed; and now my ears, too, seemed closed, the very flesh of my body seemed closed and withdrawn from all beyond it, and for a moment there was a black pocket of stillness. Deep in the stillness was. . . . what? . . . my mind, perhaps, my living daylight mind, a tiny flicker in the dark. Go back, it said. They are not here; not ahead. Nothing is ahead. Only emptiness. Only darkness. . . .

Then the flicker was gone. The stillness was gone. I clung to the rock, and the rock trembled. I raised my head, opened my eyes, and the wind beat against them with maniacal fury. The sound in my ears seemed no longer that of the wind alone, but of the night, the sky, the earth; of the very fabric of earth crumbling to sand, to dissolution.

I got to my knees; to my feet.

I climbed on.

Soon now I would fall again. . . . But I didn't fall. . . . I seemed no longer to have a body that could fall. My legs, my arms, my movements, my breathing were merely hallucinations of my darkening mind. The wind, sand and rock were hallucinations: wavering, receding, spinning, flowing: the wind and sand streaming downward, the walls of rock streaming upward, on and on, without end, into darkness. The darkness itself was an hallucination, for now, very slowly, it seemed to be fading, to be thinning—the tall blackness of rock was thinning—it was wavering, receding—it was gone. I put out my hand and touched wind. I took another step upward, and now I did fall; for there was nowhere higher to go.

I had reached the top of the pass.

I lay still. With the stillness of death. With the stillness of stone. I would not move again until the stones themselves moved; until the great wind snatched them, crumbled them, flung them in waves of sand across the waste below. I *know* that I did not move. It was simply that one moment I was lying prone and the next I was standing. Or half standing. I was crouched at the very apex of the pass, feet braced, body thrust forward, my eyes slitted against the howling blackness beyond. . . . And that was all there was. Blackness. . . . Blackness of night and streaming sand; in the sky above, across the earth below. Before my feet the far side of the escarpment fell away so steeply that no single slope or pitch of rock showed in the gulf beneath. There was nothing there: only a gulf, a void. The black void that was Karakorum.

Then the last thing happened.

The sand still blew, but I did not feel it. The wind still howled, but I did not hear it. What I felt was a presence beside me. What I heard was the thin thread of a voice.

"What do you see?" said the voice.

"I see nothing," I answered.

"Nothing?"

"I see darkness. I see blowing sand."

"And beyond the sand?"

I turned toward the voice. Dimly, in the night, I saw the seamed mask of a face.

"Turn back," said the old lama. "Look up. . . . What do you see?"

I turned back. I looked up. My eyes strained into the wind and darkness; at the nothingness that filled the darkness; at the nothingness beyond the darkness; at the thing that, as I stared, seemed slowly to be emerging out of the nothingness and the night. . . . It is an illusion, I thought. A trick of your eyes, or of your fever. . . . But it was not illusion. Moment by moment it grew larger, clearer. The storm streamed over it, but it did not vanish. The night encompassed it, but it did not fade. White, pure and eternal, it burned down into the darkness out of the black core of the sky. The bright beacon. The star. . . .

I stood poised on the rim of space.

"Where are they?" I whispered.

"They have followed it," said the lama.

"But there is no way."

"Yes, there is a way. If you have the faith, there is a way."

I leaned far forward. The wind beat at me, pulled at me. I seemed no longer to be standing on the earth, but to be suspended in space above shrieking darkness. I stretched out my hand: across the black gulf—toward the burning star.

"If you have the faith," said the voice. "*If your heart is ready. . . .*"

My body swayed. My brain reeled. The night, the gulf, the star all reeled around me, and I started to fall. I was falling, reaching out again, groping, grasping the lama. . . . Only it was not the lama. . . . I was holding a hand, and a hand held mine; it was holding tight, drawing me back, drawing me away; it was leading me, stumbling and falling, down the black funnel of the pass, and now and then a voice came up to me, but what the voice said I do not know.

Once—only once—I looked back. The wind screamed. The sand blew. The star was gone. Ahead of me, weaving in the darkness, was the faint glow of my watch dial on Khitai's wrist.

TWENTY-ONE

The rest is fragments.

There were the black boulders, the tents, the ponies. There was the monstrous tempest of darkness shrieking down from the ridge above. I was in the tent, and the tent was shaking; my body was shaking; body and mind were spinning, lost and blind, in the darkness. Then there was light. I was lying still, and Khitai was bending over me.

"Forgive me that I awake you, sir," he said, "but it is now exactly ten minutes after six."

It was later.

"They will come back?" said the boy.

"No, Khitai, they won't come back."

"Then we follow them?"

"No. There's no way to follow them."

"What do we do then?"

There was a long pause.

"We go back, Khitai. That is what they want: that we go back."

There was the base of the pass, the humps and hollows, the bare sweep of the wasteland. Hour after hour, day after day, we crept through the miles—the only things that lived or moved in all that world of desolation.

The only things except the wind. As the days passed, it no longer howled with apocalyptic fury: but it was still there, always there, humming behind us. The dark sand which it carried circled in little eddies above our heads before settling on the earth.

Then the earth spun—the sky spun—and I had fallen.

"If I die, Khitai—"

The boy spun, too, and was gone. Everything was gone. There was only darkness, great waves of darkness, a pit of darkness; and beyond the pit, at long intervals, a sound, a movement.

And at last a light. . . . At first it was very faint, very distant; but slowly it grew nearer and brighter. It was not the diffuse and lurid light of fever, but a single node of brilliance, clear and pure. It burned above the blackness of the pit—like a beacon—like a star. . . . Then my eyes were open, I was in a bed, and above me on the wall hung the Bickels' old print of the Journey of the Magi. I watched it—watched the star—until Yeng came in and put his hand on my forehead.

A caravan from Ulan Bator, said Khitai, had picked us up near the pass through the Altai Mountains. A week later we had reached Borba. Yeng had nursed me through the last stages of typhus. By mid-October I was able to get up: strengthless and wasted, but with convalescence already begun.

Then one evening the three of us sat together.

"There are some wool-merchants leaving in a few days for Kashmir," I told them. "I have made arrangements to go with them."

"You will not wait for Mr. and Mrs. Bickel?" asked Yeng.

"No, I shan't wait."

"They will be disappointed," said Yeng.

There was a pause, while I thought of how to say what I had to say next. "If—" I told them "—if after a while they have not come back—if something has happened to them—then I know—I know they would —want you to share what they have left."

Then we were at the caravan depot and Khitai was speaking. "You have forgotten this, sir," he said.

"No, I haven't," I told him.

I took my watch, which he was holding out to me, and strapped it back on his wrist.

The boy's eyes shone. He grasped my hand. "I cannot thank you, sir. A million times I cannot thank you. I shall keep it ever clean, ever shining, for all my life."

"May it be a long one, Khitai. And happy."

The caravan began to move. Yeng and Khitai waved and were gone.

Early in December, before the first heavy snows of winter, I came down through the high Himalayan passes into Kashmir. A week later I was in New Delhi, and a week after that in New York.

The two years since then have been full ones, and I have continued in the itinerant tradition of my trade. From the States, in due time, I returned to the East: first to Japan; then to Korea, Hong Kong, Indo-China, Malaya—and back to Korea. The voices grow angrier, the shadows grow longer, the white mushroom domes drift gently skyward from the flats of Nevada and Siberia. And I have had little time to think back to that strange journey through the wastes of Asia, that seems more and more to be merely a dreamlike gap in the flowing pattern of the years.

I do my work. I go my rounds. I make my calls and get my interviews and file my cables. The world is the same as ever. My life is the same as ever.

Until the wind blows.

Until it is night and I am alone in my room and in

the darkness beyond the window I hear the sound of the wind. And on those nights I turn out the light and lie on the bed and listen. . . . It is only the old fever, I think. But I have no fever. Sleep, sleep now, I think. But there is no sleep. . . . There is only the wind and the dark and, beyond them, two faint figures receding—receding—but never gone; moving on, always farther, deeper, into the black sands, under the burning star.

After tonight—after what I am writing now—I shall no longer even have the release of getting up and lighting the light and going to the typewriter and telling their story. For now I have told it. Whether the telling has brought me closer to understanding, I am not sure; and I shall probably never be sure. For where those two others have gone I cannot follow. My mind, my heart, are not ready. For better or worse, I must live my life in the world that is.

I have told all that I know, and only one thing remains. It is not a thing that I know, but that I believe, and you may take it as you will. . . . *I believe that John and Eleanor Bickel will find what they are searching for. I believe that all men will find it: somewhere, someday.*

Now the clicking keys will be silent. Night will return. The wind will return. And I shall lie in the darkness, listening, and I shall try to pray. I am a creature of my world; I do not know how to pray; but I shall pray anyhow.

For those two who have gone before us.

And for us all.